Between the Sheets

THE ANGLO ARABIAN INFUSED
ADVENTURE BEGINS...

BOOK ONE

Between the Sheets

A Story of Life, Lust and love
An Anglo-Arabian infused adventure

BRITT HOLLAND

Between the Sheets First published by Arabian Wolf Publications 2021

Arabian Wolf Productions
House of Social Enterprise BV
Geleenstraat 16,2
1078 LE Amsterdam
The Netherlands

First edition

ISBN: 978-1-8383802-0-5

www.brittholland.com

First edition Agent: Susan Mears

Contents

INTRODUCTION	9
ACKNOWLEDGEMENT	11
ARABIA	13
THE PUSSY POSSE	16
MIDSUMMER NIGHT	20
LONDON SW10	26
FLIRTATIONS & FRIENDSHIPS	31
FIRST LOVES	48
JAMES BONDING	61
LOST & FOUND	69
CHABLIS CONFESSIONS	80
MR & MRS SMITH	85
OFFICERS & GENTLEMEN	88
RELIABLE ROCK	92
CHECK-IN SHENANIGANS	96
LAP OF LUXURY	104
GUT FEELING	110
CAVEAT CARD	122
NOT MY THING	126
LIFT OFF	130
PRISCILLA	134
CHARMING COMPANY	139
REST IN PEACE	155
DATING DISCLOSURES	162

Volcanic Vilifications   178
Limbo Leisure   187
Boss-Man   194
Your Excellency   199
Ali Baba   208
O.G.S.Ms   214
Toes in the Sand   222
Trouble in Paradise   227
Pole Position   240
Best Kept Secret   245
Redhead Rebellion   250
Jessica Jeopardy   255
In the Dark   260
Omens & Signs   266
Soul Synergy   270
The Next Chapter   278
Interview with the Author   281
Also by Britt Holland   284

DM,
Thank you for your eternal encouragement and
unwavering support. You are my rock.
With my love, always

Introduction

Vivika no longer feels like her former bubbly self. She is stuck in a rut, overworked and exhausted. When a British naval ship docks in the port of Amsterdam, Vivika is compelled to attend a cocktail reception. She certainly isn't expecting to be swept off her feet by the Captain of Her Majesty's Ship *Carlington*, but a twenty-second kiss blows her mind and brings her back to living and savouring life again. When Vivika starts working for a luxury hotel chain with resorts in the Middle East, she soon realises she has joined a sinking ship. The owner, a prominent Arab businessman, at loggerheads with the management company, pins all his hopes and demands on Vivika. With an ego larger than the Burj Khalifa and a temperament more explosive than Vesuvius, His Excellency, General Salim, does not take "no" for an answer. And yet he manages to stir her in ways she had never thought could be possible. With her loyalties divided between company and owner, Vivika plots her course. Following her true north, she negotiates the waves of passion, pain, and loss. Vivika's journey of discovery brings her to encounter two very different men who capture her attention – and her heart.

Acknowledgement

Thank you to my beloved parents, Moody Blue and Daddy O', for your care, love, patience, time and encouragement always. Whether in heaven or on earth, I love you.

Thank you to my girlfriends in UAE, Jordan, the United Kingdom, and the Netherlands, for inspiring me, for your positive spirits, your input and experiences and insights.

To my two gorgeous children, and brother and sister. You are my permanent pillars in life.

Arabia

I had an up and down relationship with Arabia.

All my experiences, good and bad, had one thing in common: they were intense and unpredictable. What you saw in the Middle East was a distorted reflection of reality, much like a Fata Morgana.

The Orient has the qualities of a female temptress and those of a male magician; both sexy and elusive. The Middle-East is a region of smoke and mirrors and cannot compare to anywhere in the Western World.

In that lies its magic.

As a young woman growing up, I lived happily, in a familiar world and within a context I understood. My life was steady, apart from the usual emotional and hormonal changes that naturally occurred during my growing years. It gave peace of mind to have firm ground underfoot.

As I matured, I became interested in new possibilities and ways of looking at things. The concept of "comfort zone" became uncomfortable. I disliked routine and predictability.

As I developed, my love of travel grew. The Middle East in particular, drew me in. Like an oriental magnet, it attracted me into a thousand and one different dimensions and sensations, I had not encountered before. Some experiences were good, some bad.

To be able to have half a chance of surviving in the Arab world as a Western woman, you must have a sense of self. That self-knowledge comes with a certain level of maturity. In essence, you need to understand that if you want to take a Middle Eastern roller coaster ride, it can be scary, yet thrilling or killing.

Life in the Middle East is fast and furious, yet, at the same time, it exudes calm, mystery and seduction. If you are not yet able to handle the most challenging storms in the English Channel, then do not contemplate exploring the uncharted waters in the unpredictable high-rolling Arabian Seas. You may drown.

The Orient is complex. It is influenced by forceful factors including religion, loyalty, history, commodities, wealth, battles, greed, generosity, hospitality, hostility, magic, evil, love, killings, harsh conditions, poetic enchantment, and brutal inflictions. But the most powerful and dangerous of all is "Passion", with a capital P.

On arrival in Arabia, peace and serenity seem to envelop you. The balmy weather soothes you. The stark contrast between men dressed in white and women in black suggests clarity. The call to prayer evokes a sense of discipline.

In the Middle East, money rules, and family is untouchable. Should there be a perceived danger to either, you may have to pay, possibly with your life. Beware of thinking that you as foreigner may belong. You will never gain a place in the inner trusted circle; This sanctum is hermetically sealed, protected from parasites and contamination. Both tribe and pride are to be preserved at all times and at all costs.

If you can, avoid falling for an Arab man. They are intense and seductive. These Alpha Males are a species that seems to have become extinct in the Western world and are, therefore, exciting and intriguing to some of us. These men make you feel like a woman in the most sensual ways, but inevitably with Alpha Males comes dominance and control.

Arabs are excellent hunters. They are predators and lie in wait, tempting their prey with patience and expertise. When you are at your weakest, they move and secure you.

Unless you are made from the very DNA that runs through generations of Pirates, Bedouins, Kings, Sultans, Emirs, Generals and Rulers, you will never be able to play them at their game.

If you do fall for an Arab man and survive to tell the tale, it will be tantalising.

And so now here is my story.

The Pussy Posse

Now, before we move on to "Men", allow me to tell you about my "Girls", my "Besties", and founding members of The Pussy Posse.

Hélène was a Dutch friend who was my neighbour when I lived in Amsterdam.

Annie was British. I met her via my toy-boy, Ben, having moved to London from Amsterdam.

Within a year or two after I met Annie, the three of us, Annie, Hélène and I, joined by my brother Martin, went to Jordan. That was my first brush with the Middle East and the place where "The Pussy Posse" was born.

We did not have men in our lives; not as permanent fixtures or partners, anyway.

We were what you may describe as sassy, independent women. We all had a sense of riotous rebellion about us. We'd think nothing of jumping on a flight for a spontaneous adventure. We had positive spirits and can-do attitudes.

The Pussy Posse was our refuge, where we could share our

secrets and innermost dreams; here, we could cry and laugh. The Pussy Posse was our anchor.

Annie, Hélène and I solemnly swore to meet up twice a year. To manage our time, we agreed that one reunion should be over New Year, and the second, on or around the 21st of June, Midsummer Night.

I fondly remember our summer solstice and New Year escapades.

On one occasion, we gate-crashed the open-air opera at Glyndebourne, to watch *A Midsummer Night's Dream*. Glyndebourne is an English country house, the site of an opera house which, since 1934, has been the venue for the annual Glyndebourne Festival Opera. None of us was into opera, but we stumbled across the great place in East Sussex and thought it would be "rude not to".

In Marbella, the three of us went skinny-dipping in bioluminescent waves. It was magical—sort of like the aurora borealis, but then in the sea, rather than in the sky. We lay down on the beach in the moonlight, without a stitch on, and made "sand angels" much like we used to do in the snow when we were young.

One year, the three of us went to Costa Rica. We went white-water rafting and had fresh *ceviche* for lunch, washed down with Margaritas. We swam in the waterfall on our friend Amilcar's coffee estate. I felt rejuvenated and alive. Not only was I with my best friends, but the power of nature also impacted me dramatically. I compared the experience of being energised, to having gently bubbling Prosecco running through my veins, making me feel terrific and radiant.

During that trip, Annie laughed so much that she literally fell over in a flower bed, in the butterfly enclosure at the eco-hotel. That set me off. I collapsed, sniggering uncontrollably, next to her. Then it was Hélène who would suffer hilarity-induced loss of balance, as she joined us in hysterics between the flowers. With butterflies landing on us, we simply lay there for a while, gasping for breath and crying with laughter in the grubby soil.

One New Year, we decided we needed some Key Lime Pie. It is generally accepted that the pie comes from Key West in Florida. Whether it does or it doesn't, we decided we should go to Florida for a zesty fresh break and some of this iconic dessert. We booked our flights.

My dear boss upgraded us on the flight over to Miami. Annie had her legs crossed, sitting back on her business class seat, reading a magazine in her fully reclined position. Her foot was moving up and down. When I looked up, I saw that the guy from the seat in front of Annie had got up from his chair to put his briefcase in the overhead bin.

As he stood there, stretching up to place the case in the locker, Annie's foot was only a fraction away from his manhood. I was looking on in horror. What would happen if she were to kick him by accident? I wanted to warn her, but realised on time, that if I nudged her, she would likely spring up and move her foot to land in the middle of the chap's crotch. I decided to not say a thing. I held my breath, and thankfully, the blow was averted. As soon as the danger passed, I fell about. I told Annie what had happened. Of course, we thought it hilarious and hooted with laughter.

Hélène, who was a few seats down from us, never witnessed this sorry saga. We had not noticed, but she had slipped past us for a little "Mile-High" indulgence with the good-looking guy on the other side of the aisle from her. She was the smoothest operator between us in terms of men. Hélène always had us on the edge of our seats with her riotous stories.

But let me tell you about the Midsummer Night in the Pre-Pussy-Posse Era.

Midsummer Night

Many moons ago, I was not at all in the mood for Midsummer Night. In fact, I was not up for anything. I lived in Amsterdam. I already knew Hélène, but not Annie. I had been working my socks off and was utterly drained.

Desperate to have time to myself, I was aching to be free of any type of commitment. I was craving a bit of solitude.

That was not like me.

My friends said my energy was boundless. It wasn't, of course, but I was considered an energy junky, or instead, as I prefer to name myself, an energy aficionado.

If there was good energy around, I was drawn to it like a fish to water. But recently, I lacked my usual spark and *joie de vivre*. I used to bounce out of bed to get going with the day. But I had lost my mojo. Everything was just the same most days. Apart from my demanding work commitments, I also kept up with the constant "party routine", starting on Friday night and continuing until Sunday afternoon. The usual form was to go full out and then to crawl into bed early on Sunday night, allowing for recovery, before starting work again on Monday.

I increasingly wondered what I wanted from life. Naturally, I was grateful to be working, to be earning and to have a lovely pad to live in. I felt blessed with my friends.

I knew I did not have anything to complain about, and all to be thankful for.

Why, then, was I feeling this way? Whenever I had a rare moment of peace, my mind would wander. I sometimes, albeit rarely, thought about whether I would find a man who would hold my attention. I was very happy in my own company. I simply occasionally wondered whether there would ever be someone who I would not tire of. I always cringed when people introduced me to their other half as if they were not worthy of being whole by themselves. Why would you need someone to complete you? I believed in being bigger together, "the one and one is three" idea. What was the point, otherwise, of ever considering being a Tandem Team?

Until now, the boys I knew could not be considered men. All they wanted to do was play, impress, flirt, conquer, have their wicked way, and do it all over again the next weekend. Either with the same person or anyone else who happened to be good enough for the weekend's seamen session. It was empty and superficial. Not that I personally indulged in gratuitous sex. In that, my friends considered me conservative.

Having just come home from work, I was due to go out again in an hour. I had made a commitment weeks ago that I could not get out of, at least not at this late stage.

I may have been able to wangle an excuse had I called Edward, the British Consul-General, but the real issue was with Larissa, whom I knew I could not let down.

I guess it is the way I was brought up.

"Even if you feel you don't have it in you," my mother used to say, "then all you need to do is push yourself. Never give in to spinelessness. Show strength, Vivika."

It was an honourable sentiment. I respected my mother, as well as my dear father, for instilling values and principles in my brother and me.

However, at this very moment, I wished I could ignore my mum's words of wisdom and simply stay put and slip into my PJs. I relished the idea of a good glass of red and a relaxing movie. Instead, I went upstairs to the bathroom to freshen up. Having put my clothes into the laundry basket, I stepped into the shower cubicle and turned on the water. I moved my hand to adjust the tap, to increase the temperature as well as the water pressure. I changed the setting to massage mode and closed my eyes, standing head bowed, shoulders slumped, allowing myself to cry silently. My tears tasted salty as they rolled down my cheeks and landed on my lips. I raised the shower above my head. The water flowed over my face and washed the tears of tiredness away. Without a trace, along with the soapy foam from my body, they disappeared down the plughole. Realising that I must have nodded off, I steadied myself.

I was very impressed the first time a hand-written envelope arrived by special delivery. Edward, who my parents knew from their stint in India, had recently been appointed British Consul-General in Amsterdam. Edward did not have a wife or children. He lived in the large Amsterdam residence with his trusted housekeeper, Amelia, who had worked for him in

Lagos. Amelia moved with him when Edward was posted to the Netherlands. He became like an uncle to me.

On occasions, Edward would pick me up with his chauffeur-driven limo to go to the theatre or take me out to dinner. We enjoyed each other's company. It was an easy, comfortable friendship.

On one occasion, Edward invited me to have sushi in Okura, the Japanese hotel near to The Residence and not far from where I lived. Edward told me that, every so often, a British Navy ship would dock in the port of Amsterdam, sometimes a "mine-hunter" or a "mine-sweeper".

Edward, in his capacity as Consul-General, attended the cocktail receptions and invited several dignitaries as well as other specially selected guests.

Edward went on to ask whether I and a few of my single friends, would like to be on the "list of special invitees" when a ship was in town.

I said, "That sounds like a hoot. Yes, that would be my pleasure."

Edward replied, "Excellent, happy to hear it."

From that time onwards, I was frequently, "cordially invited" to attend the cocktail receptions, or Cocker P parties, as they called them in high society slang, onboard visiting British naval ships.

My girlfriends and I had a blast whenever we went. We were treated like ladies by gentlemen. We always had a ball, when they were in town.

That first invitation was quite something. I felt honoured and privileged. I cherished the great feeling of decadence that came over me as I RSVP'd in the third person, as protocol required.

I remembered my mother explaining what RSVP meant when I was very young. "*Répondez, s'il vous plaît*".

"It just means that you are expected to either confirm you are pleased to attend or regret and decline. But whatever your response is, protocol dictates that you do so in the third person. That may be outdated," my mother said, "but that is what is required."

I laughed. "I like things that are done in a certain way, but I also think it is very old-fashioned and weird at the same time."

My mother smiled at me. I always questioned everything and never simply took matters for granted.

The bathroom filled with steam. The turquoise and green tiles which depicted an exotic garden, graced with dainty birds, could no longer be seen.

I fell in love with the bathroom when I first saw the flat. I immediately thought of the Beatles' song that I loved, and forever associated with my very own bathroom.

I would catch myself humming the tune of "I'd like to be, under the sea, in an octopus's garden, in the shade." Situations often subconsciously prompted me to start singing or humming a song. Any little trigger would have that effect.

I eventually forced myself to turn off the shower. Dripping wet, I stepped out of the oversized cubicle.

Too tired to move, I closed my eyes and breathed deeply. With a sigh, I lifted my right leg up and placed my foot on the bidet, meticulously drying between every toe.

When I was little, my mother would always remind me;

"Dry your feet well, darling, to stop mushrooms from growing between your toes."

The idea revolted me. As a result, I always paid close attention to drying between every digit. Having finished my right foot, I exchanged feet and repeated the ritual.

The thick cloud of steam was starting to clear. I could see the contour of my naked body in the large, heated mirror.

What a sorry sight I am . Like a drenched cat, I thought.

The make-up, which I had not taken off, streaked my cheeks. Mascara-smudged eyes looked back at me in the mirror. The Alice Cooper association triggered the singer's famous song; "Here I go again."

I started humming it without gusto.

Forcing myself to get dressed, I applied some make-up and slipped into a comfortable skirt, a simple sleeveless top, a cropped jacket, and a pair of soft leather boots. It was not a particularly elegant look, but all I wanted was to feel at ease; to do what was expected of me. I would attend the cocktail reception and come back home as soon as politely possible.

I grabbed my bag and got into my car. I put my key in the ignition of my Golf and set off to pick up Larissa. We continued towards Amsterdam harbour, where the officers of HMS *Carlington* were ready to welcome us.

Had it not been for Larissa, I may well have decided to stay at home. But I forced myself, and I went.

The encounter that followed changed my life forever, on that Midsummer Night, when I met James.

London SW10

Both Annie and I lived in Southwest London. In Fulham, London SW10, to be specific. I had worked in the travel industry for quite some time now.

I was now employed by an airline in the UK. I had the good fortune to travel often to fantastic places. At that time in my life, jumping on a plane was like catching a bus.

I had reached a senior leadership position reasonably early on in life. It was a combination of clicking with my new boss, him seeing my potential and being in the right place at the right time.

One of the best things about my manager back then was that he let me get on with things. He trusted me to do the job. That sense of support made me fly higher than I could have imagined. If someone believes in you and says that the space outside the box is the area on which to concentrate, then I can relate and be my best. Paul didn't stifle me. He just constantly mentored, nurtured, encouraged, and humoured me. Paul was the person who gave me wings to fly and soar early on in my career.

He understood my sense of individuality. He enjoyed good repartee, and I rated him as a "proper person"—people with good energy and real stories to tell attracted me. I gravitated towards those individuals who had guts, determination, and a love of life. And Paul was one of those people.

All these and other qualities were found in one of my very best friends; Annie. She was an outrageously talented TV producer. With her mop of blond hair, bright blue eyes, quick wit and sharp humour, Annie was what you would call "good value".

We both shared a love of travel and property investment. We both felt stifled by routine. Whenever either of us felt stuck in a rut, we would call each other and talk it through. We would do some scenario-planning and find a way to get the oxygen flowing again, no matter what change may be needed.

We delighted in our joyful and colourful existences. Our lives were uncomplicated in that we were "mostly single", had good incomes, were young and bold and didn't shy away from challenges or adventures. In fact, we embraced them wholeheartedly.

Annie was introduced to me when she returned from a long-term work gig in Australia. She was a close friend of Benedict's older sister, Anya, or "Onions", as Annie used to affectionately call her.

I met Benedict in London when I first moved to England from Amsterdam. Ben was four years younger than me. We got on like a house on fire, and we spent a lot of time together. Ben was a brilliant blessing and great fun. We went on camping trips, fishing expeditions, jaunts to Cornwall and day trips to France.

Not only did I hugely enjoy Ben's company, but he also stopped me from thinking about James, whom I still desperately missed. Over a few months, Ben and I became Friends with Benefits, or Friends with Benedict. Basically, he was my toy-boy plus and a wonderful guy.

One spring evening, Ben and I were at a party at our friend Charles's house.

The theme of the party was; "What you were wearing when the ship went down".

Ben was donning tropically themed swimming trunks and a necklace of dried chicken bones around his neck. I was wearing a halved and hollowed coconut as a bra, which Ben had cleverly made. We were both sporting grass skirts. My costume was topped off with a flower garland and bright yellow shell-shaped earrings. The big, dried bone in my hair was generously donated by an Islamic butcher in Balham. Pebbles Flintstone would no doubt have approved.

Though the weather was sunny, the temperature dropped dramatically during March evenings. But we were committed to entering into the spirit of things, so tropical dress it was. To brace himself for the cold evening air, Ben wore his donkey jacket and I had put on my camel coat. We slipped them off by the door, where the pile of other "Shipwreck Party-Goers Coats" were accumulating as more and more people arrived.

We were drinking Pimm's, which seemed to be appropriate in our tropical island-themed party. If truth be told, we were always swigging Pimm's. Even during winter. It was just such an excellent drink.

We were chatting away when Annie made her entrance. She came in through the back door wearing faded jeans, a white linen shirt, sparkly flip flops, and a big bright torch strapped on to her forehead.

"Well, put flippers on me and call me a duck, quack, quack", Ben exclaimed.

"If that isn't Annie Fanny. Where have you been, you old cow?" Annie walked over to Ben, laughing. She hugged him. Keeping him in her embrace, Annie firmly pulled him into her chest. With his nose between her boobs, she fondly patted his head and then soundly spanked his bum, over the top of his grass skirt.

When Ben was able to come up for air, he said "I had no idea you were back from your travels. Great to see you, you saucy Belle. You look great. But what the hell is that light on your head? What does it have to do with the theme of the party?"

"I came as a lighthouse," Annie laughed. "When the ship goes down, they will all be looking for me. And here I am. To save your souls."

Annie took a step back from Ben.

While holding his hand, she looked him up and down. "Benji-Ben, bloody duck, you have dried up nicely. Can't believe you were simply Onions' little brother. Look at you. It seems that you have entered into the metamorphosis stage from boy to man. Not an unattractive one either, I may add."

Turning her attention to me, Annie said, "Hello, and who are you? Are you and Benzi-Dicky-Liscious together?"

"Benzi-who?" I laughed. It was impossible to get annoyed with this positive spirit, even though her questioning was outrageous. Had circumstances been different, I may well have seriously put this intrusive stranger in her place. But she was cool and bubbly. I instantly liked her.

Annie's long blonde hair tumbled down her shoulders and was her crowning glory.

"I think that lion's mane on your head needs a bevy of some sort. And that bright guiding light needs some fuel, I have no doubt" I said. "Let me get you a pint of Pimm's, while you chat with Benzi-Dicky-Liscious."

In response, Annie threw her head back and roared with laughter.

"Thanks, that is so nice of you. You sound like a Sister-in-Arms to me."

Then, turning to Ben, she said, "You chose well Ben. She seems fab."

Flirtations & Friendships

We flew over Cyprus. Once we reached the shores of the Mediterranean, the pilot set in our descent over Jerusalem. We continued towards Amman, the capital of "The Hashemite Kingdom of Jordan".

Hélène was flying in from Amsterdam and would meet us there.

We were all trying to peer out of the window as we were coming into land. There is something about new places, especially when you arrive at night. The lights of the homes and the streets give the darkness a glow, but you cannot see beyond. The promise of exploring a new place is thrilling. Even if you have read up on the place, you will never know what destiny holds when you are there.

Although I travelled quite a bit, I had not yet been to Jordan.

For some reason, the Middle East had always held a fascination for me.

Countries in both Asia and Africa were considered Arab states. From Morocco to Oman, from Sudan to Iraq, the Arab member states spanned continents.

I always felt there was a mystical quality to the Middle East. Other regions did not hold the same appeal, but this part of the world had somehow attracted me since I was a lot younger like no other region had.

The Moroccan Arabic spoken dialect is very different from that of The Levant, which is where Jordan, Lebanon and Syria are located.

I found it all quite fascinating. The whole region was considered "Arabia", yet the differences between the Arab states were quite varied in many ways.

Jordan, I had heard, was less "strict" than some other countries, yet was naturally steeped in Islamic traditions and culture. I was excited to spend the week ahead in this new place.

"I wonder whether La Belle Hélène will be at the hotel when we arrive," I said.

"I would have thought so," Annie answered. "She arrived from Amsterdam quite a while before us. Hélène will be well ensconced by now and no doubt waiting for us to rock up."

"Don't be so sure," I chuckled. "You don't know Hélène yet. She doesn't like to hang about. She will have checked out a Mall, or gone for supper somewhere," I said.

Annie and Hélène had not yet met, though, of course, knew of each other's existence. They would be sharing a room. I would share with my brother Martin.

We checked in to our interconnecting rooms. Hélène was not there, though her luggage was.

"She probably went off to enjoy her time," I said.

We unpacked our things and went for a bite to eat in a place close to the hotel.

When we came back a few hours later, Hélène was still

nowhere to be seen. Martin was about to investigate where she may be when we heard a loud and rhythmic knock. Martin jumped up and opened the door.

There she was. In all her splendour. Hélène.

True to form, she was dressed in cream, tan and navy blue with a splash of colour. She never failed to wear an exquisite silk scarf, tied around her blonde bob. Hélène always looked as if she was going into elegant combat, usually, with a cigarette between her lips.

Smoking hot.

"Martin," Hélène squealed, "how lovely to see you!" This was followed by, "Vivi, how are you, darling?"

Then she spotted Annie, sitting over on the sofa.

"You must be Annie; how nice to meet you. Finally. We will be sleeping together this week. I look forward to that immensely." Hélène's English was excellent. But she was unmistakably Dutch.

Very direct in her way, Hélène did not care for formality. Annie got up and gave her a hug and said, "I am looking forward to sleeping with you too."

"You are funny," Hélène laughed heartily. They were clearly going to hit it off.

Martin opened the complimentary bottle of red wine in the room.

"Pass me those two wine glasses from above the minibar, please, Viv," he said.

As we were four, Martin went into the other room to fetch two more glasses.

"Where were you, Hélène? We were expecting to find you here when we arrived," Annie said.

"No," Hélène laughed, "no time to waste. Never sit around waiting. Get on with life and allow it to happen."

"Now I understand what you meant by me getting on with Hélène, Viv. She totally shares the same vibe."

Then turning to Hélène, Annie went on, "Always great to meet a fellow Life-Lover."

And then to me, Annie said, "Good work, Queeny, for bringing us all together."

We made ourselves comfortable on the beds, and Martin lounged on the windowsill.

Hélène settled down to regale us with her adventure of the day. As was her signature, Hélène elaborated in detail. Whether it was an exact rendition of what happened, we would not know, but we were ready to hear Hélène's version of events.

"May I smoke?" Hélène asked.

"Do what you have to," Annie laughed, "just spill the saucy beans."

Hélène lit up a cigarette and settled into telling her story.

Having arrived, Hélène decided to have a drink in the lobby of the hotel.

With some hours to kill, she went down to people-watch and relax after the flight.

While she was sipping on a glass of wine, a well-dressed gentleman managed to engage Hélène in conversation. He wore a smart dark suit and crisp white shirt.

He looked as if he was about to leave the lobby, Hélène observed. As he got up, the good-looking man glanced over at Hélène, casually picking up his jacket and mobile phone. He then walked over to Hélène and introduced himself as "Michel".

Hélène was used to getting attention from men. She had a

magnetism which drew them towards her. She exuded both confidence and beauty. With a laissez-faire attitude about her, Hélène appealed to most members of the opposite sex.

She epitomised class and smiled easily. She had travelled and lived all over the world.

Hélène knew how to rely on herself and loved new situations.

Michel asked her where she was from. She didn't answer his question.

Instead, she laughed spontaneously and said, "Michel; that is not an Arabic name".

"It is," he said, "many men are called Michel."

He appeared taken aback by her response but was instantly engaged.

"Why not Ahmad or Ali?" Hélène laughed. She was teasing him and testing his response.

"Were your parents French, and they got lost in Arabia? Perhaps you are Lebanese."

"Wow," Michel flashed his charming smile. "You are one hell of a pretty fire-cracker." Quickly followed by, "May I sit down?"

"Yes, sure, sit if you want to," Hélène said, somewhat dismissively.

Michel joined her for a glass of wine. After half an hour or so, he said, "Well, dear beautiful lady, we Jordanians are known for our hospitality. Allow me to invite you to dinner. You would be doing me a great honour."

Michel's expensive-looking mobile phone had been vibrating on the table repeatedly. He had not answered it.

Now, he picked it up and simply pressed a single button for instant connection.

"It is Michel," he said. "I shall be with you in fifteen minutes.

Prepare my table. I shall be joined by a most lovely lady."

A short pause followed. Then Michel continued, "No, it is not my wife. This lady is much more attractive and intelligent." Michel winked at Hélène.

"My table. In fifteen minutes."

Cutting the call abruptly, he turned back to Hélène. Charm personified, he asked, "My lady, would you like to use the bathroom before we go?"

"No thanks," Hélène said, "I am all set."

Hélène felt she had hit the ground running. She was ready to start her Middle-East adventure.

Having spent the lion's share of her childhood in Qatar, Hélène knew some Arabic. In the spirit of things, she gathered her stuff and said, "*Yallah*, let's go."

Michel eyed her and smiled.

"I am looking forward to this promising evening," he said. "If nothing else, I am sure we shall have quite a lot of fun.

After a tedious day with my fellow shareholders and visiting investors, I am certainly thrilled to have made your delightful acquaintance."

"Flattery will get you almost anywhere," Hélène flirted, in her outrageously confident manner.

He settled the bill and offered his arm to Hélène, which she took.

The staff were fluttering around Michel as if he owned the place. Maybe he did.

Hélène continued.

"Michel's car was parked outside with its winged doors open. *Ja*, like in one of those Bond movies." She hooted with laughter. "Michel was standing by, waiting for me to get in on the passenger side.

After I sat, he leaned over me and strapped me in, like he was securing me," she chuckled.

"He walked round to the driver's seat and started the engine. He revved it loudly. I think he was sending me a message. I felt like I was sitting on his powerful roaring thing." Hélène cackled and stubbed out her cigarette. She immediately lit another.

According to her story, Hélène and Michel arrived at the restaurant "La Maison Verte".

This appeared to be an upscale and hugely popular restaurant, frequented by the well-to-do, including businesspeople, politicians, Ladies that Lunch and Girls that Gossip.

Hélène said she loved the place from the moment she arrived. She painted a picture of how the twilight sunset caught the stained-glass panes in the Art Deco awning, saying they looked like sheets of bright emerald. Dimly lit, adorned with exquisite lamps, the restaurant instantly appealed to Hélène. With its pristinely starched tablecloths and comfortable seating, she described the atmosphere as being like that of a very high-style French Bistro. Everyone appeared to have a cigarette or cigar in hand. Hélène was pleased that she could relax, without worrying about whether she could light up.

"I will order," Michel said, "but if there is anything you wish for, let me know. I already told them to bring me my wine, from the selection I keep here. A Red. You will love it as much as I do, I am quite sure." He winked at her.

"I recommend the excellent succulent steak, medium rare, with pink and juicy meat at the centre."

He then leant back to see how Hélène was going to handle his innuendo.

"Yummy," Hélène whispered seductively.

"Pink peppercorn sauce to enhance the exquisite cut," he continued.

"You have such style and taste, Michel," Hélène egged him on.

"You are a pretty special girl. Funny. Smart. And a ravishing beauty. *Al hamdoolilah*. Praise the Lord."

Hélène took a cigarette from the pack on the table. She placed it provocatively between her full and glossed lips. Her lipstick was just enough to be sexy, yet not enough to be too much—more Grace Kelly than Marilyn Monroe.

Quick as a flash, Michel produced his flame, to light her up.

Men, though they tried, could never control Hélène. She was in charge. Just as the fire started raging in the loins of defenceless men, she would make her decision either to play with them like a cat with her mice, or, to send them packing with their totem pole erect between their legs, lust still stirring and their urge unsatisfied.

Hélène was clear and decisive when she reached that point. Just like with her cigarettes. With her lipstick still freshly on them, she stubbed them out and left them to smoulder in the proverbial ashtray.

"They are all *Mudda Fuckas*," she said in her blunt and straightforward Dutch way.

"If you don't use them, they will use you."

The way Hélène treated any male was a reaction to an earlier relationship.

Years ago, the man of her dreams cheated on her, shattering all her illusions of a Happily Ever After.

Therefore, Hélène packed her bags and left their Malibu

home. In addition to the trauma of deceit and separation, she had to leave her beloved kittens behind—two fluff balls of love and affection. Being robbed of her babies broke her heart. Never again, she promised herself, would she put her happiness in the hands of a man.

Hélène maintained that no man could ever be trusted. As a result of her pain, Hélène proceeded to use men like consumables that could be enjoyed or ditched, depending on her appetite.

As dinner progressed, Hélène pulled out yet another cigarette, which Michel swiftly whipped from her fingers. He back-flipped it through the air, to land it, perfectly positioned, in his mouth, a smooth move he could not afford to get wrong. Michel lit the cigarette, inhaled deeply, got up and walked around to where Hélène was sitting across the table.

People were turning to see what was going on. Michel planted his lips on Hélène's while gently nudging them open. Hélène, cool as a cucumber, sucked the smoke from his mouth, into hers. She then raised her dark lashes and looked at him, and slowly exhaled, blowing perfect circles into his admiring face.

Having infused Hélène with some sexy cheekiness at La Maison Verte, Michel ordered a second bottle of red Cabernet- Sauvignon.

"I love that wine," he said.

"It is so rounded and full, and unsurpassed in bringing out the flavour of delicate pink meat. Let me top you up. This wine is like the best oil, to make you feel physically on top of your game."

He was on a roll, clearly fully limbered up.

"From your hand, I would not refuse the finest of liquids, nor the creamiest of sauces," Hélène responded. She was enjoying the outrageous flirtations and handsome, attentive company.

She could see Michel stirring. He repositioned himself in his emerald-green velvet chair. The pressure in his active volcano was visibly building. Hélène was enjoying being in charge and pressing his buttons.

For dessert, Michel allowed Hélène to choose.

"The sweet things have to be selected by the lady," he said. Hélène opted for Crème Brûlée, which they shared.

Michel cracked the glaze of burnt sugar on top of the delicacy. He scooped out a spoon of the creamy, deep yellow, custard-like mousse, with specs of the vanilla seeds clearly visible.

Michel, satisfied that he was getting the attention from the fellow diners, proceeded to put the mousse in his mouth. He softly sucked off a tiny bit of dessert while looking at Hélène in a sultry fashion. He then took the spoon out of his mouth and popped it into hers.

Hélène, enjoying it all thoroughly, played along and closed her eyes. She allowed some of the now-runny liquid to escape her lips. The sauce trickled down to land on her breast.

After an almost full display, she scooped up the spill off her bosom with her little finger. While smiling at Michel, she purposefully popped her pinkie into her mouth and sucked it clean, with a look of total divine ecstasy and fulfilment on her face.

Hélène knew that her impromptu act had been executed to perfection. Murmurs in the restaurant rose. An older lady, dressed in crimson, turned puce, and gasped audibly, which simply encouraged Hélène to keep up her performance.

Hélène clearly turned Michel on. She unmistakably recognised the look of lust in Michel's eyes, giving away his desire to continue the evening with her. He suggested coffee at his house.

"I have Arabic sweets to tempt you, My Lady."

He went on to describe them oozing the purest of honey and the freshest of nuts. Hélène knew full well that stickiness and nuts were nothing to do with baklava. The description was merely coding for sex.

"He was so easy to decipher," she laughed.

She recounted, stepping up her outrageous flirtations and said, "*Ja,* Michel, you are James Bond, and I am Pussy Galore."

Hélène hooted with laughter as she recalled her over-the-top flirtations.

Michel and Hélène left the restaurant. Michel pulled out ten Jordanian Dinar from his wallet and tucked the note into the hand of the valet. The car doors were already open, the engine running.

When they arrived at the house, Michel opened the gates by remote control.

He parked outside the beautiful wooden, heavily gilded front door. Giant semi-circular steps, carved from black and white marble, led up to the opulent hallway.

"Good evening, Sir, Ma'am," the staff welcomed them.

In the middle of the massive dome, spanning the hall, hung a large and elaborate pale pink crystal chandelier, the size of Hélène's Fiat 500. Underfoot, Hélène was enchanted by the most glorious extensive mosaic floor. It depicted beasts, winemakers, lions attacking gazelles, flowers and the tree of life. Hélène asked Michel how long it had taken to make the floor.

"I don't know," he said, "it was lifted from an ancient church and put in my hallway. It is the genuine article. I don't like anything pseudo. My wife is fake enough. I am a lover of antiquities, apart from my spouse. She is an antiquity, but not of great value. Not anymore, at least."

Hélène looked at him.

"Michel, you can't say things like this about your wife."

"Why not?" he replied. "I was brought up Christian and what I said about my wife is God's honest truth." He winked at her. "It also comes in handy to have a Christian background in Jordan. It qualifies me to have this church floor in my house.

It would be odd if it was sent for safekeeping in an Islamic household. It belongs under my roof. Thankfully, I have friends in all the right places. They give me excellent antiquities, and I do what I can for their welfare. That is equality in my books. Fair and balanced. Treat thy neighbour as thyself. We scratch each other's back."

Putting his hand in the small of her back, Michel then told Hélène about the fountain, positioned just under the dome. He explained how it used to be part of the nymphaeum at one of the Roman sites. Michel said that him agreeing to have these centuries-old antiquities in his private house was considered a magnanimous service.

Under Michel's watchful eyes, robbers could not steal these precious relics. Incorporated in the grand hallway of his lavish home, they were forever safe in his custody.

Hélène was fascinated by the way antiquities were owned by those with wealth and *wasta*, which is an Arabic word, that loosely translates to "who you know".

Using one's connections to get things done is part of the culture in the Middle East.

Achieving results through favours, rather than on merit, is typically considered entirely acceptable. At least, that seems to be the case amongst those who benefit, and those who are in charge.

The opinion of anyone else appears to be of no consequence. Michel invited Hélène into his library. She sat down on the comfortable, three-seater Chesterfield. Michel took a cigarette from the elaborately decorated silver box on the table and lit it for Hélène. He selected a cigar from the humidor, cut it with a special silver tool and used a black lacquered torch to ignite it. It was quite a ritual. The coffee arrived minutes later.

Hélène and Michel chatted easily while sipping the fresh brew, which smelt divine. The coffee was blended with cardamom and served in little Arabic coffee cups. They looked like small bowls, which you could comfortably hold in the palm of one hand. When both were empty, Michel inverted Hélène's coffee cup. He placed it on to its saucer and left the coffee sludge to dry. He proceeded to read her cup and spell out her future—a very Arabesque fortune-telling method. Hélène, according to the dark brown markings, would be gloriously spoilt. As fortune would have it, her future would involve recurring meetings with an attractive Arab.

"The name of this special man begins with the letter M," Michel said.

With a knowing wink, he took her hand and pulled it into his lap, while caressing it.

"*Ja*, and then I felt his *thing*." Hélène roared with laughter. "It was a big one," she went on, "a very Arabian Stallion". It was ready to run the race. For sure, he wanted me to saddle up and ride his pony," she said in her bold and Dutch way.

We all cracked up.

Hélène explained to Michel she had to go back to the hotel, as we would have arrived by now. He told her that he realised he could not persuade a woman who was waiting for her arriving friends to spend the night with him.

"Naturally, I wish to have incredible sex with you. It is a big shame for you and, of course, also for me. But you need to meet your friends. Definitely, we will do it next time."

"He did not say that!" Annie exclaimed.

"Come on, Hélène, that is taking things a bit far," I said, almost sliding off the bed laughing.

"I swear he did," Hélène insisted.

"So, that was it?" Martin chuckled.

"Well almost," Hélène said, "but he wanted to "give me something to remember him by"."

"Oh Lordy, what did he mean by that?" Annie said.

Wide-eyed, we listened on.

Hélène explained.

Michel said that since he did not have the opportunity to make love to her, he would leave Hélène with the memory of him. Next time, she would be able to enjoy his incredible performance.

Michel summoned the maid to fetch her farewell gift. On unwrapping it, Hélène was surprised to find the most luxurious, fluffy, sumptuous bathrobe she had ever seen. She gasped and said, "Thank you so much, Michel. It has been an utterly fantastic and positively memorable first evening in Jordan. I so enjoyed my time with you."

"Me too," Michel said. "Next time you come, you must stay and swim with me. For now, promise me that every morning when you wake up, you get naked. After your shower, promise me that you put that lovely body of yours in this robe, and think of me."

"I certainly will," Hélène smiled demurely. "Every morning, I will think of you."

Michel called for a car which Hélène recognised as a Corvette. They zoomed off back to the hotel, where he had first picked her up. Hélène French-kissed him right outside the entrance, under the admiring eyes of the valet and head concierge. Without looking back, she took the elevator up to the seventh floor where Annie, Martin and I were waiting for her.

We had the most fantastic week in Jordan. The local people were so hospitable and kind. Everyone was keen to speak to us, invite us for coffee and even to meals in their houses and for tea in the desert.

The country blew us away. The Rose Red City of Petra was astonishing; our overnight camping in the vast Wadi Rum desert was indescribable. Floating in the Dead Sea, due to its high levels of salt which stop you from sinking, was a very surreal experience. My favourite was plastering our bodies and hair with the million-year-old mud, rich with minerals and healing properties.

We had such a great time, but after all the fresh air, hiking, and new impressions, we were totally bushed.

Having arrived back at the hotel, all rosy and snoozy from a day in the Rift Valley, we decided to eat in and have an early supper. We took a seat at the poolside Italian restaurant. There was a table that was adjacent to ours. The woman, who we later learnt was Rania, caught my eye and smiled at me.

"We hope you don't mind," she said, "but my friend Lama and I are thirsty for some European-infused company. Would you like to join us for a bottle of wine?"

We were all up for it and accepted their spontaneous invitation. We pushed our tables together to make one large one. The staff in the restaurant helped us to rejig our seating and brought us complimentary sweets.

They were all smiles, and so were we.

On the evening we first met, Lama and Rania gave us tips on where to find the hidden gems in Amman. One of their insider recommendations, was "La Maison Verte".

We chuckled, and Hélène, bold as a butterfly, regaled them, in a nutshell, about her evening with Michel, in that same restaurant. Rania and Lama told us that "the high society in Amman" loved to gossip. They indulged us in a bit of local hearsay too, as it related to Michel. It was light-hearted and not malicious. None the less, it painted a picture of what went on in West Amman Society.

Apparently, Michel, whose surname started with an H, I don't recall the full name, was married to one of the most elegant and wealthy women in town. Michel was one of the richest men in Jordan. He had a reputation with the ladies.

Lama told us that Michel owned a luxury apartment in one of the residential towers. Other wealthy prominent males of Amman's high society did precisely the same. They, too, owned flats in the same building. Their mission was to seduce and conquer the limited pool of "willing women". Some were romanced into their beds. Others were given handbags, trips and other gifts or money, to land them between the sheets.

Organised, undercover infidelity and promiscuity, it appeared, was rife in Amman.

Hotel owners picked up on the opportunity. They were now investing in the development of "residential units", also dubbed, "Man Caves". A new lucrative market, ripe for penetration.

"I must say that it seems Michel was very taken with you, Hélène," Rania said. "He would not usually take anyone home, even if his wife were out of town. I expect he will be dining out on dinner with you for a very long time".

"You are a lovely, beautiful woman, Hélène," Lama said and came around the table to give her a hug.

It was touching. Somehow, both Lama and Rania understood that Hélène's bravado was born out of pain, vulnerability, and insecurity. Only a sensitive woman's soul would realise that.

It struck me once again how important it is to have women who have your back, who understand your pain and who rejoice in your success. Thank God for Annie and Hélène. They were my best buddies, my sisters-in-arms, my rocks.

When, much later that night, Martin went for a run, Annie, Hélène and I acknowledged the amazingness of the gift of girlfriends. We ordered a bottle of bubbly to be brought to the room and made a toast to each other. We raised our glasses.

"To being friends through thick and thin," I said. "Through sick and sin," Hélène added, which made us crack up. "To The Pussy Posse," Annie completed the toast.

"To The Pussy Posse," we repeated together.

And with that, The Pussy Posse was born.

First Loves

It had been a while since I had spoken to Lama and Rania. It was great to still be in regular touch. They were due a trip to London. I could not quite make out what was going on, but one way or another, Lama and Rania were not able to come over. Lama said there had been a strike.

I remember thinking that going on strike did not seem to be a very Middle Eastern thing. Only later did I realise Lama may have meant that there had been an "air-strike", as in warfare. I never found out. In context, it was not important. The fact remained; they were not able to come to London.

It was Lama who suggested we connect virtually. She sent an email with the subject, "We need to catch up". She went on to say, we should ignore trouble and strife, or trouble and strike and that we must celebrate life whatever it throws at us. "I will set up the call on Skype if you like," I responded. "Do you have a preferred time?" I asked.

Annie and Hélène were travelling but said, go ahead anyway. Lama and Rania did not have a preferred date.

"OK, then mark your diaries for the 21st of June, at 11.11

Amman time" I wrote back to Rania and Lama.

"And before you ask, yes, on midsummer's day, it is perfectly acceptable to drink wine before noon". I ended the message and sent it.

We all made sure we were "plugged into the mains" and had enough "grape juice" on standby. Lama and Rania met up at Rania's creative studio in Amman, so they were together.

After some fond hellos and general banter, Rania was telling us about the time when she studied art in Florence and dated an Italian guy. Rania told us that they used to share more than a pizza, and how he had shown her some "previously unexplored places of interest" which her Jordanian parents most definitely would not have approved of. For a considerable period, Fabio was the statue of David that had come to life for her. She was smitten with his charming attentions and Italian ways.

We ended up talking about our first loves.

From my London lounge, I saw Lama pouring the red wine into their oversized crystal glasses.

"I propose a toast," Lama said. "Cheers, to us, and those we have loved before."

We raised our glasses and acknowledged each other online. We then settled down into "mode".

"You go first, Vivika," Lama continued. "If we get bored with your love story, we will jump back to Rania or me."

We all laughed, ready to share and enjoy our Skype session. "Tell us about your 'Favourite First Love', Vivika," Lama said. "Who was he?" Rania asked. "When did you meet this special man?"

"Well, ladies," I started off, "not only is this one of the top men I have ever met, but you also may not believe it when I tell you, that I met him all these years ago, on this very day."

"What? That is unbelievable!" Lama shrieked.

"You've got to be kidding us," Rania whispered.

"You have to tell us from the start. Go, girl!" Lama said.

"I am not going to breathe another word until you complete your story."

I started off by briefly telling Lama and Rania about the parties on the naval ships. I explained a bit about the cocktail receptions my single girlfriends and I had been to and how we always had an enjoyable time. I then went on to say how, on this particular day, I did not want to go, but I was compelled to.

I started the story of my "First (grown-up) Love".

"Having picked up Larissa, we arrived in Amsterdam harbour. I parked the car on the quay next to the massive naval ship. We made our way up the gangway and were greeted at the door of the Officers' Mess.

As it was summer, we didn't have coats with us and therefore skipped the wardrobe formalities.

"What can we get you to drink?" the welcoming officer asked. Without much ado, I politely said I would like a "Horse's Neck".

The officer in question looked at me slightly flummoxed but recovered quickly.

"Ah, you have been on Her Majesty's ships before, it seems."

A broad knowing smile spread across his face. He introduced himself as "Officer David".

Even though he seemed like an amiable sort of chap, I remember trying to avoid getting into a conversation. I just was not in the mood. I was tired and feeling out of sorts. I apologised and went off, leaving Larissa to talk to Officer David.

I can't say I am proud of my behaviour. I was in one of those impossibly recalcitrant moods that you should have outgrown by the time you are seventeen. Clearly, I had not.

The Horse's Neck did the trick, though, and chilled me out a little. I went over to Edward, the Consul-General, to greet him. He was a wonderful gentleman. I always enjoyed seeing him. Edward introduced me to some people, and then to a girl who worked for the British Tourism Promotion Board. I can't quite recall, but she held a post with Visit Britain. Then he excused himself, to circulate and mingle, as any good Consul-General would.

The woman Edward introduced me to, Victoria, started talking and did not stop.

She had just met the Captain of the *Carlington* and appeared to be instantly smitten with him.

"Oh, he is so amazing," she said. "He lives in Dorset. He has two golden retrievers, and they have just had puppies, how darling is that? He's travelled all over the world. His three sisters all went to the same school as I did. Such an amazing high-brow educational institution," she drawled. "Only the cream of the crop is accepted."

Wow, I remember thinking, *what arrogance. If Miss Visit Britain represented "the best", things were speeding downhill at a rate of knots.*

Just at that time, the Captain joined us.

"Well, good evening," he said, "and welcome to HMS *Carlington*."

"Thank you," I responded.

Instantly, Miss Visit Britain popped her perky bosoms forward and fluttered her eyelashes. The Captain did not seem to notice, or perhaps he didn't care.

He held out his hand to me and said, "And whom do I have the pleasure of meeting?"

"Vivika," I answered. "Who are you?"

Of course, I knew he was the Captain, and in charge, but as I said, I was in "one of those moods".

"I am the Captain of this vessel," he said "Captain Bowen-Jones. James Bowen-Jones."

He was tall, blond, and handsome, with bright blue, intelligent eyes.

I looked across and there, in an alcove on one side of the Officers' Mess, Larissa and Officer David were snuggly sitting alongside each other, giggling, on the built-in bench, next to the built-in table. Everything was built-in to avoid chaos when on the high seas. Anything that was not pinned down securely could go flying and cause injury, I realised.

David caught my eye and gestured for me to join them. I excused myself from the Captain and Victoria, which delighted Victoria, and left them to chat.

I sauntered over to where David and Larissa were sitting.

"I am just showing your friend the oceanographic map. Would you like to join us?" Officer David politely asked me.

"No, thank you. Don't let me interrupt your studies of the ocean floor," I smiled.

"I just wanted to make sure Larissa was OK. I can see she is in good hands."

We chatted for a bit. When I considered it not too rude, I excused myself.

Having turned on my heel, I almost bumped into the Captain. "Here you are," he said. "You did not appear to wish to have a chat with me. Perhaps you would like me to show you around the ship? We can go on a tour."

I could not muster any enthusiasm but didn't have an excuse either, so said, "OK."

"Jolly good. There are a few more people who would like to come with us. Wait for me here, and I will be back in two minutes."

David and Larissa also joined, more out of respect for his boss, I would say, than out of interest. Officer David's attention was on a different topic.

The group gathered, and we set off. We climbed the narrow stairs up to the bridge.

From high up on the deck, there was an impressive vantage point of the whole harbour of Amsterdam.

Captain James was talking about a recent voyage and some trouble they encountered when all the men were taken ill. They were quarantined off the coast of Malta.

Sounded grim. And smelly. A ship full of men with the runs. Yuck, such an unattractive thought.

Everybody was listening intently to Captain James Bowen-Jones, except for me.

My eyes were wandering. I spotted a car driving along the quay.

The Dutch Police force was known for their incognito Golfs when they needed to be inconspicuous and work under-cover. Ironically, most people were aware, so in reality, not so "under-cover".

I could see a guy looking up at the ship from within the passing car.

His eyes were steely blue. I grabbed the microphone, which

was within reach, right next to where I was standing. Just to entertain myself, I guess, I said, "Hey, Blue Eyes."

I had, of course, not realised that this naval intercom system was designed to communicate across vast expanses of water. From the top of the mine-hunter, my words bounded through the air, ricocheting back and echoing across the port.

I was taken aback, as even I could see this uncalled-for action was totally inappropriate.

Captain Bowen-Jones looked me in the eyes, then took the inter-com, or whatever you call the maritime broadcasting mic. He fixed his gaze on me and firmly, yet politely, said, "Let's go back downstairs, shall we?"

I felt somewhat embarrassed, I must admit. I had definitely overstepped the mark.

What was I doing and what was I thinking?

Trying to recover, I looked him up and down and said, "Oh, you really think you're something, don't you?"

He didn't flinch.

"Look at you," I continued. "Such a shiny clean blond attractive thick mop of hair, all handsome in the sunshine. Look at your shimmering shoes, they almost look like patent leather. And what about all those stripes and even wings on your sleeve and shoulders? Wow, very swish and impressive." And then under my breath, "No wonder Ms Britain fancies you. She has her heart set on 'That handsome Captain'."

His mouth twitched. Was it anger? A suppressed smile? I couldn't work it out.

"Shall we?" he said and planted his steady hand gently, yet firmly, in the small of my back.

I don't think anybody noticed, but I felt his command.

Intriguingly enough, I did not seem to mind.

I am Miss Independence and don't take kindly to authoritarian gestures. But on this occasion, I meekly went downstairs. I recall taking note of my almost submissive response. *Unusual.*

Whenever a crew member passed the Captain, they saluted him, with "Evening Captain". Even if Captain James had already passed, they would spring to salute him and stand to attention.

Wow, I thought, *he certainly seems to command the respect of his men.*

When we came back to the Officers' Mess, Captain James said, "I am going to the heads, and then I will be back."

"Going to give head, Captain BJ?" I blurted out.

My bemusement from a few moments ago had clearly passed. I was back to being outspoken and uninhibited.

"No," he said. "I am going to pass water, as is nature's wish. Then I am going to wash my hands and have a drink and a chat with you. For your information, the heads are the loo on a ship."

Off he went.

I was planning to tell Larissa that I would be leaving and that if she wanted to come with me, she would be very welcome. Or, if she preferred to keep studying the seafloor with her new teacher, that would be entirely up to her.

But the Captain had just mentioned that he wanted to talk to me, so it would be a little off, to say the least, to simply slip away. Even I was not that rude, no matter how recalcitrant I felt on that particular evening.

When Captain James re-appeared, I was about to say goodbye. "Where are you going?" he asked.

"I am tired, and you too must want to sleep having entertained all these Viper V.I.P.s, excruciating ex-pats, dire diplomats and me, my friends and I."

"No, not at all," he said. "I believe you owe it to me to apologise for your demeanour just now, up on the bridge and, therefore, you can hardly turn me down for a gin and tonic, wouldn't you agree?"

Captain Bowen-Jones did not wait for my response and pointed to a place for me to sit. I followed his order. He took his seat next to mine. He then signalled the waiter in a way that must have been sign-language for "two gin and tonics, and make them strong, on the double, please", as, within what seemed like seconds, two pint-sized glasses of G&T arrived.

"Good health to you, Vivika, it is my great pleasure to make your acquaintance," Captain James said.

I realised I had had my fair share of drinks. I was rather tipsy by now. In boozed-up fashion, I responded.

"To you and all who sail in you, Captain. To absent friends. To those who went before, to legends of the fall and freemasons of the future."

I proceeded to take a swig of my G&T and looked him defiantly in the eye.

"Now then," Captain James said, "what is this boisterous nature of yours? I am intrigued and would like to understand what flipped your switch and ruffled your feathers today. I am sure you are normally a ray of sunshine. However, it seems you are in a rather rebellious mood, if you don't mind me saying so."

"To be honest," I said, "I wasn't wanting to go out tonight, no offence, Captain. And then, when I arrived, Miss Britain started gushing on about you. Such boring rubbish. But anyway, I am glad to see you have me worked out and understand how I tick." I was picking up the pace and was on a roll. I started talking, being cheeky, rambling on, until, unexpectedly, Captain James stopped me in my tracks. I was holding court with my legs crossed and swinging my left foot provocatively in his direction. He looked me straight in the eye and poured about a third of his gin and tonic into my boot. My sock was soaking, and my toes were sopping wet.

My eyes shot open. I looked at Captain James in disbelief. "What did you just do?" I said.

"I put some G&T in your bossy boots," he replied. "You needed a little calming down. That's all. Now, let me take you outside to empty your boozy boot for you."

I remember thinking, *You fully understand how to handle me.* That was very rare for anyone, and it threw me off balance.

"You are nuts," I muttered under my breath.

With my foot stirring and shaking the gin and tonic, there was nothing else for it, but to do, what the Captain suggested. On the deck, outside the Officers' Mess, he stopped and said, "Lean on me for support." He bent down to take off my boot.

And with it off, I stood there like a numpty—one shoe on and one shoe off.

My imaginative brain took over. I found myself humming the children's tune, "Diddle, diddle, dumpling, my son John, went to bed with his trousers on, one shoe off and one shoe on, diddle, diddle, dumpling, my son John".

This old nursery rhyme popped up and hurtled me back to the days of sitting on my British grandmother's lap, as she taught me nursery rhymes and read me stories. Captain James heard me humming the melody.

"That reminds me of my grandmother," he said. "She taught me that nursery rhyme."

What are the chances of that? What a crazy world, connected by grandmothers who never met, on a ship that hunts mines, with a Captain who has just emptied part of his gin and tonic into my boot, at a cocktail reception on a naval vessel, I did not want to be at. All very surreal.

Not helped by my Horse's Neck and gin and tonics, I realised.

"Where are you from?" I asked

"My father was British and joined the Navy, just like generations before him. My lovely mother was born in Scotland and educated in England. They met when my father was a young naval officer. My mother was the daughter of a diplomat, and she was invited for a "Cockers P" cocktail party, with some of her girlfriends, just like you were today.

"Isn't it time we slipped your boot back on?" the Captain said.

He kneeled in front of me and produced two small plastic bags from his pocket. Captain James peeled off my wet sock while I steadied myself on his shoulder for support.

He popped the offending item into one of the bags, and then took his crisp, clean, white folded handkerchief from his other pocket, which he used to dry my foot and in between every single toe.

He then slipped my now much drier foot into the other plastic bag so that it would slide into my boot.

"Where did you get these plastic pouches from?" I asked. "Were you planning this operation all along? Did you come prepared?"

Captain Bowen-Jones was still crouched down. He looked

up at me, with his handsome smile and perfect teeth.

"It is all about scenario-planning, my dear. It is my job to anticipate events and put energy into achieving the desired outcomes." Then he stood up.

When he was fully erect, so to speak, he didn't ask, but gently drew me towards him, kissing me expertly on the lips.

Right there, on the deck.

I responded without resistance. I got lost in the Captain's kiss, which cannot have lasted longer than twenty seconds, yet it seemed a divine eternity.

I remember exactly how I felt when it happened. My stomach ricocheted seven decks down into the water of the Amsterdam harbour and then travelled the same journey in reverse. I was totally taken aback at my response to this unexpected and unforeseen interlude.

I was trying to recover my position. Captain James held my gaze as if to steady me.

"I need to go," I said.

"That is OK. But on one condition."

"Condition?" I blurted out. I clearly sprang back to my default mode of flippancy to overcome any possible insecurity or embarrassment.

"Who are you to put any conditions? I don't take orders from anybody."

"Not an order, more of a kind request," he said.

"Allow me to take you out to dinner tomorrow night. Let me spend some time with you and get to know you better. I would like that very much indeed. Would you do me the honour?"

"No," I said. "Definitely not. Not in a million years."

"Why not?" He looked surprised and intrigued.

"I have never gone out with anybody within seventy-two hours of meeting them. It is a rule of mine."

I have no idea where I came up with that and why, but that is what I said, and I was sticking to it.

Larrisa and I said our goodbyes and off we set, down the gangway of HMS *Carlington*, on Midsummer Night, many moons ago."

James Bonding

"I must be boring the socks off you," I said to Lama and Rania. "Keep going," Lama said, "I am lapping it up and learning as I listen. That Captain displayed some mighty fine insights and some gutsy moves too."

Rania jumped in. "Don't stop now, Vivika. I am utterly enchanted and totally gripped."

We laughed and replenished our glasses. I continued.

"Next day Larissa and I were in the office, looking a little worse for wear, but none the less, on time. We settled into our work.

Larissa was clearly bursting to talk about the previous night, but as our boss was in the open-plan office, she was forced to contain herself. As soon as the manager, Menno, a pretty spineless Mr Blobby, closed the door behind him, Larissa gushed, "Oh, my goodness. Last night was *zo ongelooflijk*, so unbelievable, meaning "amazing" in this context."

"I am glad you enjoyed yourself," I smiled.

"OMG," Larissa swooned, "Officer David is just to die for. I cannot stop thinking about him in his uniform and the way he looked at me. Let us call the ship, Vivika."

"What do you mean?" I said, "Why do you want to call the ship?"

"To talk to Officer David, of course. I am desperate to hear his voice. I am totally smitten with him. I have the number of The *Carlington*. David gave it to me. He was so sweet and so handsome. I want to see him so badly."

Larissa dialled the number. I heard her say, "I am calling for Officer David."

Then, after a minute or so, she turned to me and said, "It is the Captain. He wants to talk to you."

"Why?" I asked. "Whatever for? I thought you were calling David."

Larissa looked at me pleadingly and said, "Captain James said he is prepared to put Officer David on the phone, but only after he has spoken to you."

"Ah, for goodness' sake," I said, grabbing the telephone. "Hello." I said, "Vivika here."

"Hello, Vivika, Captain James here. I wondered whether you might allow me to take you to dinner tonight."

"What did I tell you?" I said.

"I will not have dinner with anyone within seventy-two hours of meeting them and you, my dear Captain, are no exception."

"Look," he said, "we are in port for five days and I want to spend them with you."

He continued, "Please allow me the honour of having dinner with you. Then you decide whether or not you too would like us to spend the days ahead together."

Larissa was hopping around. I felt sorry for her, so said, "OK,

Captain, you have a deal but only if you are joined by all your officers. How many do you have?"

"Twelve," he said.

"OK, bring them all. Tonight, we will be at your ship at seven o'clock. I will make the reservation. And don't pull a fast one. If there are fewer than twelve officers, the dinner is off. Is it a deal?"

"You are a tricky one," he said, "but yes, we have a deal."

That evening, we went to a restaurant named "Bali". It was located across the floating flower market in the centre of Amsterdam. They knew me well as I often took guests there for work. I reserved a long table and ordered the well-known traditional "Rijsttafel", a nearly unending parade of small plates, all filled with different spicy-sticky-sweet Indonesian food.

On arrival at the restaurant, we gathered around the elevator which takes guests to the first floor where the restaurant is located. It does not fit more than four people at the same time. All I remember is being in the lift with two or three other people and Captain James. He leaned into me and whispered in my ear, "I am sitting next to you."

I felt weak at the knees. My tummy turned a *salto mortale. How can I eat anything at all after that?* I thought.

Captain James's presence affected me, there could be no doubt about that.

We arrived on the first floor. As the lift doors opened, the team who I knew so well all rallied round and said, "Good evening, Ms Vivika, so lovely to see you. Come, sit at the long table. Welcome."

I sat next to Captain James. It felt lovely to be so close to him. He was a marvellous conversationalist. Attentive and charming, alert and with a great sense of humour. He was telling me wild stories about his time in the Navy as well as dirty jokes, elegantly recited. He thoroughly entertained me and captured my attention.

After the main course, before dessert, I wanted to wash my hands and excused myself to go to the loo. As I rose from my chair, not only did James get up, but every one of the twelve officers around the table.

What the hell, I thought.

"What's going on?" I whispered to James.

"Don't worry about it," he said. "It is simply "the done thing" to stand up when a lady leaves the table."

I chuckled under my breath and made my way to the bathroom.

When I came back, all the officers and Captain James rose to their feet again and remained standing until I was seated.

"That was embarrassing," I said to Captain James.

"Why?" he asked, "We can be as foul-mouthed and cheeky as we want, but in the Navy, we will never compromise on manners and protocol."

"Double standards," I laughed.

"No," he said, "that is simply how it is. There is no compromise on etiquette in Her Majesty's Service."

After I sat down, James leaned over and whispered in my ear, "I want to stay at your house".

"Excuse me?" I said, looking at him.

"I want to stay at your house," he repeated.

My breath caught in my throat. "You want to do what?" I faltered.

Captain James held my gaze as he looked at me, intently.

He repeated his words.

"I want to go home with you tonight. I will go stir crazy on that ship, knowing that you are so close by, yet not with me. I cannot think of anything more wonderful than to spend the night with you."

I was stunned.

He slipped his hand under the table and stroked my knee.

"Take me home, Vivi," he whispered.

After dinner, some of the lads went off into town to enjoy Amsterdam's bars and nightlife. Officer David and Larissa went "for coffee". Captain James and I returned to the ship to pick up his things.

Around ten minutes later, James arrived carrying a plastic bag. We made our way down to my car.

"What did you bring?" I asked.

"I will show you. First, let us get into the car."

We got in. Then, Captain James put his hand into the bag and pulled out a pair of running shorts and a toothbrush. Next, he retrieved a dark, almost black, slick looking, hard-covered case. It looked like a modern mini tool-kit.

"What is in that? Did you need to bring your tool kit? Are all your bits functioning OK? Do you have all your screws, or were you hoping I could give you one?"

I thought I was witty until James pushed a small release button.

There, in front of my eyes, was a firearm. One of those guns that is silent. What you may call a "concise killer kit".

"Why are you carrying a weapon? Who are you? Captain James Bond?"

"Just in case," he said.

"There has been a spot of trouble in Germany, related to the IRA.

We have been advised to be vigilant. Not sure if you noticed, but we were shadowed by a police escort from the moment we left the ship."

I looked bemused. "Really? So, that policeman in the Golf on the quay whom I saw, when I used the maritime intercom, was an undercover cop?"

"Bright as a button you are, Vivi. As intelligent as you are sexy; I like that."

He grinned, closed the case, and put it back into the plastic bag.

"Do you know this music?" he asked while slotting a tape he took out of his pocket into my casette player.

"I was at their live recording. Mark, the lead singer of Level 42, gave this tape to me."

"Wow," I said because even I knew who this band was.

The label of the cassette, with a hand-drawn smiley face, read, "Cheers Matey Boy. Wot Prats. Wot a Laugh".

I didn't ask, and he didn't say. We enjoyed the music and chatted easily. We continued our way to my house, which was in the leafy outskirts of Amsterdam.

As we were driving along, I asked Captain James whether he was married.

Better check, I thought. A bit late in the proceedings perhaps, but still, I needed to know.

He looked at me and said, "I am in a state of separation."

Relieved, I pumped up the music. After a little while, James reduced the volume and put his hand on the back of my neck and caressed it, saying, "I like what I see, and I am very privileged to be in your exquisite company."

He said it in a flawless Scottish accent, sounding precisely like Sean Connery in a James Bond movie. I couldn't talk. He noticed and smiled.

We drove in silence for the next ten minutes or so until I parked the car and invited him into my Amsterdam pad.

Apart from that first night at my place, we stayed in a deluxe hotel in Amsterdam.

Several weeks earlier, I had won some prized vouchers for several nights at one of the five-star hotels in the city. In my job, it was not unusual to be given "incentives" from hotel partners. We did a significant amount of business with them, and this was their way of "keeping us keen and coming back". I had not thought much of my free stays, but now they came into their own.

The next day, I made reservations.

James and I entered the vast, lavish suite, overlooking five converging canals.

We drank champagne. We indulged in fantastic food, as well as every inch of each other.

One night, we had a barbecue with all the officers, Larissa, and me on the deck of the *Carlington*. The contribution, courtesy of "Her Majesty," was English sausages and booze. This was the second meal we had with all the officers there. It was great fun. They let their guard down, took out a guitar and we sang to The Beatles "Love, Love, Love" and Gloria Gaynor's "I Will Survive" and many hits that we all knew off by heart. That week in Amsterdam, James and I spent all of our days and nights in each other's company. Our time together felt genuine, full of positive energy and utterly heavenly.

On the day before the ship was due to leave port, James and I were driving across Dam Square.

At the traffic light, he looked at me and said, "We stopped the clock. We truly stopped the clock, Vivi."

He took my right hand, turned my palm upwards and kissed it. James gently folded my fingers over, leaving his kiss as a keepsake, to hold in the palm of my hand forever.

Then the lights turned. I swallowed and tried not to cry. I had never felt such an affinity with anyone before.

Not ever.

"Well, ladies, there you have it. "My first grown-up love". All those years ago.

Now I nominate one of you lovelies to spill your beans."

"Listen," Lama said, "you cannot possibly cut us off now. We are hanging on your every word. Rania, what do you say?"

"I say we continue. I will die if I don't hear what happened next. I need the loo, though. Are you OK if we have a sanitary stop and pop the cork on our next bottle?"

Having agreed to reconnect five minutes later, we paused our Skype call.

"Make sure you don't go anywhere, and that you pick straight up where you left off, Vivika," Lama said.

Lost & Found

L ama, Rania and I reconnected. I settled back into recounting events, all those years ago.

I was distraught when Captain James left. My heart was broken.

I needed space, air, and oxygen. I just wanted to go off for a drive in a car with the roof down.

In the past, I owned several convertibles. They were never the latest models, as I could not afford them, but they always gave me a sense of freedom.

Going for a drive with the fresh breeze on your skin and wind in your hair is such an excellent way of clearing your mind, I always thought.

At the time of meeting James, I owned a bog-standard Golf.

Feeling so utterly distressed and depressed at his departure, I thought that a convertible may do the trick and somehow allow me to feel better.

I decided to go to the local car dealer. I scanned the showroom and the forecourt but could not see any convertible cars. The owner of the dealership, whom I had met in the past, walked up to me.

"How may I help you?" he asked politely.

"I want to buy a convertible. Not a new one and not at huge expense, but a convertible, none the less."

The owner confirmed my observations. "I don't have any," he said.

Clearly noting my disappointment, he said, "Tell you what, I may have something for you. Why don't you take a seat?"

I sat down and wondered what the dealership owner had in mind.

He walked over to his desk on the other side of the showroom. He fumbled about in the top drawer.

He pulled out a little pile of photographs and came back over to where I was sitting. He sat opposite me. Then, he placed a stack of pictures face down on the table in front of me.

"What do you think of this?" he said.

I turned over the photos, and there, beaming up at me, was the most perfect, funky, gorgeous character of a car I had ever seen. It was metallic baby blue, with a black top, black tires with white rims and a sport-sized steering wheel. The connection with the car was instant.

"Why are you showing me these pictures?" I asked.

"Well, talking to you, it made me think you may be interested in buying my wife's car. We are installing a new kitchen. That little venture turned out to be far more expensive than expected. Frankly speaking, if this kitchen is to go ahead, the car will have to go. Are you interested?"

"Yes," I said. "Yes, I am. She is perfect."

That evening I went over to see the car, which was parked in their garage.

What a blossom of a car, I thought.

We agreed on a price and off I went, roof down in the classic Volkswagen Beetle Karmann convertible.

I named her "Blossom". I associated Blossom with James in every single way.

Life went on, with Blossom to take me places. She made me think of James every day. Not that I needed reminding. He was never far from my thoughts. I remembered our incredible time together, the way he treated me; how he made me laugh and made me feel; how we spent five days in a perfect bubble.

"You know what, girls?" I said to Lama and Rania.

"I often remember that day when I met James. I was so desperate not to go for drinks, and to stay in my comfort zone, at home.

As it turns out, that 21st of June was the most significant point in my life. Funny how things turn out. Things always seem to happen for a reason."

"After this amazing meeting of souls, did you ever see your Captain again?" Rania asked.

I continued.

"Months later, with James never far from my mind, I was inspired by the event of *Sinterklaas*. It is a time of celebration and tradition in The Netherlands.

I decided it would be an idea to send a unique parcel to the BFPO (British Forces Post Box) address. I did not know if the package would arrive.

I bought some traditional sweets, *marsepein*, *pepernootjes* and dark, white and milk chocolate letters. You usually buy just the first letter of the name of a person you want to gift the chocolate letter to. But I purchased twelve chocolate letters, spelling "CAPTAIN JAMES".

I figured all the twelve officers could have one of the letters that made up his name.

I threw in an extra deluxe version of the letters C and J for good measure, clearly intended for Captain James himself and marked especially for him.

I added a poem, as is also tradition, along the lines of; "Dear Captain James and your fantastic crew, we loved having you in Holland and hope you did too. Life goes on, we know that much, but there are times when we feel, we should stay in touch. In the Netherlands, we are celebrating the St Nick occasion, and we thought you should too, whatever your location (I know, shoddy rhyming). So, we send you, with love and without further ado, some presents to remember us, as we do you too".

I bundled it all into a package and took it to the post office. I crossed my fingers, hoping it would arrive.

James continued to live on in my mind, my heart and my dreams. Whenever I was with Blossom, I felt James's presence. I would talk to him in my head and share a joke with him. His sense of humour was epic and his ability for hilarious banter unsurpassed. Merely thinking of him amusing me, or vice versa, would put a smile on my face, and relieve my aching heart.

I continued with my job in the Netherlands. I was finding the role to be monotonous and repetitive. Clearly, a change was needed.

As I loved to travel, I applied for a job with an international airline company in the Netherlands. I successfully went through the interview process in Amsterdam and was then told that this role would be transferred to the UK. The company HR director asked me whether I was still interested. I confirmed this and landed the job with the British branch of the airline. The post was vacant and needed me in it as soon as possible.

I packed up my belongings, having secured a room in a flat in Fulham, in London.

I set off in a very fully loaded Blossom, by ferry, to the UK. On the day I left the Netherlands, there was a powerful storm.

Making it through heavy rain and high gale force winds, I finally arrived in London.

Blossom's convertible roof became dislodged on that journey, due to the forceful weather. From that day onwards, the rain came through the gap between the top and the windshield, leaving me soaked whenever I drove in a downpour.

Happily, the airline supplied me with a company car for my sales job, and Blossom could be taken out on sunnier days.

I flew all over the place and travelled the country extensively, meeting clients and finding new prospects. I was out most of the time or "on the road", as we called it.

When travelling around, I often recalled my time with James and wondered where in the world he might be.

I truly felt we connected on another level. I could not imagine that I would never see James again. My gut could not stomach the thought of it. My mind did not allow me to think of it.

I tried to forget about James and tried to cherish the unforgettable memories of our unlikely encounter. He could not compare to anyone else.

But it seemed it was not meant to be. Sad and challenging

as it was.

I poured my heart into my work.

The time I spent alone, driving up and down motorways, allowed me to think and try to heal from the heartache and loss. I had to face reality.

The airline's UK organisation was relatively small, compared to their set up in Amsterdam.

After some sales calls one day, I returned to the office to do my follow-ups.

Patricia, the admin manager, said, "Vivika, you received a call."

"Ah, thanks," I replied. I always had messages on my return to the office.

"The call came from The Royal Yacht," she informed me.

"Excuse me?" I said.

I had no idea who that might be.

Was this a sales lead I should be following up on? It sounded unusual. However, I managed a wide range of clients, so it could be a simple explanation related to my work.

Rory McLoughlin, one of the sales team, happened to be in the office. He was a young, keen professional and one of the rising stars in the team I managed.

"Well, Boss," he said, "are you taking over the Queen's Household, Royal Yacht and all?

If they have that colossal yacht, why would they want to be flying our airline? Or is there something else you should be sharing with us, Boss?"

"That is enough cheekiness from you, Rory," I laughed. "You owe me a report."

"Aye, Aye, Captain," Rory joked.

He was a great guy. He would go far.

"Talking about 'Captain'," Patricia said, "the person who left the message, was actually the Captain of the Royal Yacht'.

Patricia paused for Rory and I to appreciate her inspired link to Rory's "Aye, aye, Captain" comment.

"Here is the number the Captain gave me."

Patricia handed me a bright yellow sticky note. I looked at it. "Who did you say called, Patricia? What is the name of the person?" I asked.

"The Captain of Her Majesty's Yacht," Rory interjected. Presumably, even Queeny's ship only has one Captain?" He was teasing me.

I mockingly shot him a stern look and said, "I expect your report on my desk before the close of business today, so you best get on with it."

With that, I left the sales office and went off to my own domain, down the corridor.

I couldn't think what the Captain of the Royal Yacht might want.

I was about to follow up on what I presumed was a sales lead when a huge and beautiful butterfly landed on my desk. I had no idea where it had come from. It sat there quietly for a while and appeared in no hurry to fly off. It was mesmerising.

I pondered the mystical magic of transformation.

One day you are living life as a bog-standard caterpillar, munching through the leaves to fill your day.

Over time, as you mature, you intuitively "cocoon".

It is not a process you choose or would consciously know how to perform. It is an inner compass that guides you, an evolvement that "cannot but happen". It occurs by the grace of nature.

The cocoon may look bland and dull from the outside. But on the inside, an utterly magical metamorphosis is taking place.

Shedding off the remains of primary being, you emerge, renewed and resplendent and able to fly.

A whole new life of possibilities and opportunities awaits you. You are now able to soar to new heights. You can see the top of the flowers from the sky, rather than from the grubby soil. Anyone's life can become transformed by events.

Metamorphosis happens to us all as we develop and grow.

As I completed my random thought, I opened the window to set it free.

The boldly coloured butterfly flapped its delicate wings and took off. With purpose and without hesitation, the creature appeared to know intuitively where it was heading and took flight into the outside world.

I zoned back into the moment and looked at the bright yellow note with the telephone number, which Patricia had jotted down. Before calling, I decided to "have a cuppa", as the team used to say. It had been a long day. Some tea and biscuits were a welcome thought.

I went to the kitchenette down the hallway and prepared my tea. I came back to my office and placed a steaming hot cup of Earl Grey and a few custard cream biscuits on my desk.

I had been in the car pretty much all day, so I stood and exercised my legs a little.

While standing, I dialled the number on the post-it. The phone rang and was answered after the first ring.

Very efficient Royal Naval Household you have there, dearest Queen E.

I asked to speak to the Captain.

"Please allow me to enquire as to who is calling."

I answered, "Vivika Baron".

"Thank you, Ms Baron". The elegant-sounding male voice on the other side of the phone said,

"The Captain is expecting your call. Bear with me, please. Connecting you now with Captain Bowen-Jones. Please hold."

I reeled in disbelief. *Captain Bowen-Jones? As in James? What was going on?*

After a few rings, I was connected.

"Vivi!" James exclaimed. I could hear his smile down the phone.

"I am so happy to have located you. It took me some time but I found you."

I was so baffled I could hardly speak. I could not believe I was talking with my favourite man on the planet, who I had pretty much given up on.

"How..." I managed to stammer.

"Never you mind, Vivi, I have my ways. I may be a bit of a scoundrel, and I know I have not been in touch, but ever since we received that fantastically creative and hugely appreciated Saint Nick's gift from you, I have put some effort into finding you. With a bit of help from my friends, I traced you. How the devil are you?"

"Oh my God," I said. "I can't believe it's you. Got to say this is a bit surreal and you caught me totally off guard. I thought you were a sales lead."

Then I laughed.

"I am so happy to hear from you, James. How are you doing?"

"I am doing great, Viv. Can't wait to catch up. Let's meet."

"Where are you?" I asked.

"We are in port, in Portsmouth. Come down. Can you make it tomorrow?" James asked. "What do you think, Viv?"

"Rude not to," I replied.

It was an expression James first used when I met him. It appealed to my sense of humour, and I had used it ever since.

"Good call, Viv. Excellent. How does around noon sound? I will pick you up from the station. Will you be coming down from London?"

"Yes, I will be."

"OK, let me know which train you will be on and what time you get here."

"Sure," I said.

"Take this number, store it on your phone and keep it with you. It is worth gold dust, as it has me on the other end of the line."

He chuckled, then in the same Scottish accent, he said, "See you tomorrow, Gorgeous Girl."

He rolled the "Rs" appropriately, and with great emphasis. Then he hung up.

I could not stop beaming. It was like my face was going to split in two. I was ecstatic, over the moon, giddy with delight and every other expression that eloquently described an "utter state of bliss".

"Thank you, God! Thank you for hearing my prayers."

I so wanted to see this man again. And now I would. James had found me, and I was not planning on losing him again.

The following morning, I caught the train to Portsmouth.

As we pulled into the station, I saw James from the window,

waiting for me in the sunshine.

When the train came to a full standstill, the doors opened and I alighted.

There he was.

He looked tanned and gorgeous, wearing his signature chinos, white and pink check shirt, dark blue blazer and tan leather shoes.

The sun shone on his clean blond hair. The breeze lifted it like it had that first day on the bridge of the *Carlington*. He looked both dapper and debonair. I remembered now how nice and tall he was. A certain authority seems to come with men who look fit and are around 6 ft 3 or about 1.92 m, depending on where you come from.

He spotted me and came running towards me. He opened his arms wide and embraced me. James hugged me warmly for some time. Then he took a step back and looked at me.

"Wow," he said, "you are a sight for sore eyes. You look wonderful, Vivi. What is your elixir?"

I smiled and we hugged again. This time, James planted a kiss on my forehead.

"I am so thrilled to see you. Thank you for coming, Viv".
"Thank you for finding me," I said.

"With some help from my buddies in the force, I located you and for that, I am one happy man."

He smiled warmly.

We were both instantly at ease. James held my hand as we strolled out of Portsmouth train station.

Chablis Confessions

"Now then," James said, "I know a nice place overlooking the Solent. Let's find a spot with a view so we can settle down for a proper catch-up. We have some chatting to do, don't we, Viv? The place I have in mind is on a bank, overlooking the sea. What do you think?"

"Sounds good," I said, "but we need a drink."

"We do, my dear, we do. We will get some on the way."

We headed for the off-license and went in.

"Do you have a corkscrew?" I asked James.

"Don't worry about opening the bottle. I have my ways," James said and winked at me.

"OK," I said. "But I am thirsty."

"Me too," he smiled and shot me his "and horny too" look. My stomach did a tumble.

We walked down towards the coast and sat down on what looked like a grass-covered dune. It was quiet with nobody around.

"So, Hotshot," I said.

"Hmm, you are still your good outspoken self, I see." He smiled.

"Did you expect someone quiet to turn up?" I asked.

"No, and happy to hear and see you after all this time. On excellent form and in fine fettle as I remember you. Could you pass me that wine, please Viv?"

I passed him the bottle. James started to take the leather lace out of his left boat shoe.

"Now then, watch how it is done," he said. I looked on sceptically.

He took the seal off the chilled Chablis and pushed the cork into the bottle.

"I don't like corks floating in bottles," I said.

"Neither do I," he replied.

James proceeded to make a knot in one end of his leather shoelace. He lowered the knotted lace into the neck of the bottle and positioned it underneath the cork.

He proceeded to gently wedge the cork upwards, using the small knot as its lever.

James controlled the whole operation perfectly. He teased the cork out through the neck of the bottle until it was released.

I was, to put it mildly, wildly impressed.

"How cool are you? That is utterly spectacular handling of the situation. I forgot how resourceful you are."

"I will remind you how resourceful I am," he said and made it quite clear what he meant by that. With a twinkle in his eye, he asked, "Wine, Madam?"

"Yes, please, Sir." I whipped out two plastic cups the chap in the off-license had given us.

We opened the jar of olives we had picked up and started talking as if no time whatsoever had passed.

James told me that he was now the Captain of Her Majesty's

Yacht, HMY *Britannia*. He regaled me with stories of his recent travels and where "he and the boys" had been since our time in Amsterdam. He told me about Officer David and how taken he was with Larissa. Until they arrived in Stockholm, that is, where another lovely blonde had taken his fancy.

After an hour or so, with the bottle finished, he said, "Let's go for lunch."

I realised I was quite in the mood for a bite to eat. "Good idea. Where shall we go?"

"I know a great place for fish. We will have to behave, as they consider themselves elegant, but the food is worth it. It's just a short walk away."

We set off and wandered towards the restaurant, in the direction of the port.

James told me a bit more about their recent visit to Stockholm and suggested that I should meet him on their next visit there.

I recalled the situation of him revealing the gun to me in Amsterdam and asked if he had ever killed anyone. He tapped his nostril with his right index finger, like some sort of undercover agent who knew the answer but was not at liberty to share it.

We arrived at the restaurant, which was indeed elegant. James ordered the seafood platter.

"Would you like to stick to Chablis for continuity," he asked, "or would you prefer to try something else?"

"I want to stick to what I know and love." He knew I was not merely referring to the wine.

"Good call. Why change anything if we both want more?" Throughout the afternoon, he ordered another bottle or two.

I told James he was the reason for me buying Blossom. He

was charmed and said he looked forward to meeting "Blosh" soon. His immediate nickname for the car made me laugh.

"You are the dad. You were the one who planted that seed, so yes, it would be great to introduce you one of these days." "I am Blosh's proud father," he grinned, "and I can't wait to make her acquaintance."

After a good few hours of catching up, James said, "Viv, I need to tell you something."

He looked serious. My heart sank. It was clearly something I was not going to like.

"Tell me," I said.

"Well, when you met me and asked whether I was married, I said I was in a state of separation."

"I know," I said. "Are you back together?"

James continued. "It was neither elegant nor right of me. I used the term "separation" in a naval context. Being separated does not mean that a couple is no longer married, legally separated, or divorced. It just means that I was at sea, and we were separated. But my wife and I are together, though obviously, we don't see each other for long stretches at a time."

I forked my shrimp and pushed it around my plate, dipping it in the sauce but not eating it. I didn't know what to do. I am not a homewrecker, but James lived in my heart. And now I had seen him again, we were as good as we were in Amsterdam. I was confused. I simply said, "That was wrong. Now, what am I to do or say?"

"Say or do nothing," he said, "apart from curse me. I regret being dishonest and am sorry that I was not in touch sooner. And I am thrilled to be here with you now."

"Me too," I said.

I could not deny it. Whatever James said, right here and right now, could not take away from the fact that I was with him and felt complete.

Mr & Mrs Smith

By the time we finished our lunch, people were arriving to have dinner.

At around 9.45 p.m. James said, "Darling girl, it has been amazing, but I guess I need to allow you to catch the last train to London. It would be a bit much to smuggle you on to Her Majesty's Yacht, but you must come for dinner with my officers soon."

He settled the bill, and we set off for the station. By the time we got there, the last train to London was just pulling out.

"That early, how is that possible?" I exclaimed.

"This is not 'the Big Smoke', Viv. These are the provinces."

"I never thought to check. I am so used to London where services run twenty-four hours a day," I said.

"It happens, Viv. Not to worry. Let's see what we can find for the night'.

We set off down the street through a pretty Victorian neighbourhood, in pursuit of a place to stay. While strolling along, we spotted a Bed & Breakfast sign in a garden filled with fragrant roses.

"Listen," he said," I know I am due back on the yacht, but I will make a phone call and tell them I am dealing with an international challenge. If they need me, I am not far away so we should be OK."

We went in. As we entered, a bell rang. It was one of those contraptions that catches the top of the door once it opens and makes a sound.

An older lady, in her late 70s, came out and took her place behind what can only be described as a lectern.

"Good evening," she greeted us curtly.

I could understand that the landlady may not be too amused as it was close at 10.30 p.m. and rather late for a check-in.

"Good evening to you," James said. "We would like a room for the night, please."

She looked at him and said, "I only have one room left."

"We only need one room," James said, smiling in a cavalier kind of way.

"It is a single room. It only has a single bed," the lady replied. "We will take it," James confirmed.

The woman looked at him, took her pen and her registry. "Name?" she asked with apparent disdain.

Without hesitation, James looked her straight in the eye and said, "Mr and Mrs Smith."

The woman sternly handed James the key. Hanging from it was a hefty metal tag with the number 2 on it. She took the money and left us to our own devices having said, "Up one floor, second on the left".

The minute the woman disappeared behind the door from where she had come, I couldn't help but burst out laughing.

"Old grey-haired stroppy biddy," James said. "She needs a

good seeing to."

"James, I don't think it is on the cards for her."

"Maybe not," James laughed, "but I hope it is on the cards for the other lady in my company." With that, he held my hand and led me up the sweeping staircase to the single room.

We laughed, kissed, and made love.

Officers & Gentlemen

"Did you see each other again?" Rania asked.

"We did," I replied.

"Tell us what happened," Lama urged.

"After our reunion, James and I stayed in touch. Whenever he was in port in Portsmouth, I met up with him. James was introduced to Blossom and greatly approved of her.

When James came up to London for business, and the weather allowed, we put Blossom's roof down and cruised across London. We ventured out into the surrounding countryside for a pub lunch or walk.

Blossom was more than just our transportation. She represented our bond and the adventures we shared.

One day, James rocked up at Oxford Circus. We went for pizza in a place just off Berkeley Square. While having lunch, we were totally absorbed in conversation.

A couple interrupted us.

The man said, "We could not help notice what great repartee you have between you."

James looked at me and I smiled.

"Join us for a glass of wine," he said, which they did.

We spent five hours in the pizzeria, chatting and laughing. We then said our goodbyes and sauntered off towards Regent Street, slightly boozed up.

As we walked past the House of Garrard, which was the Crown Jeweller at the time, James said,

"Let's go and take a look."

He took my hand, and we walked in.

The salespeople were on high alert. Loved-up couples are good potential customers.

James left some space between us. He then raised his voice and said, "Darling, is there anything here you like?"

Now the staff were ready to pounce.

"Really Darling?" I responded.

The salespeople were drooling at the prospect of a killer sale. They were gathering around. James came back to me and put his arm around my shoulder.

"Darling, what would you like?"

"I would love a pair of earrings," I replied.

"Let's see what they have here, my queen; you are in the right place," James said as he planted a kiss on my lips.

At this, the salesperson whipped out the earring tray and placed it on the counter. Another two trays followed.

James was in full swing now, pointing out ones he liked. I dismissed them all.

"I just want ones like you gave me, the ones with the diamond-studded hoops, and pearl droplets. But I can't see them here," I said.

With that, James thanked the staff for their help and said, "Well then, my queen, off we go."

The guard bade us farewell politely as we exited.

I whispered to James, "I could have totally ruined you."

We laughed. James knew me well enough to play this game and to enjoy the drama for them and the giggle for us.

"Let's catch a movie," James suggested, as we passed by the cinema on Regent Street.

They were showing "Basic Instinct", the latest box office hit, featuring Sharon Stone.

We did not see much of film. Let us just say that Sharon Stone's "beaver" was not the only one getting the attention in the cinema that evening.

If James happened to be in the UK on the annual occasion of the London Marathon, he would run it.

One year, he entered it with his close friend Fredric, who was blind.

They were connected by an elasticated contraption and ran in parallel.

After the Marathon, James and Fredric were invited to Buckingham Palace for tea, because of James' line of duty. James was firmly linked to the government, Buck Pal, the forces and any authority you could imagine. I never asked. Nothing of that mattered to me. Only James did.

When Fredric was introduced to the Queen, James said, "Commander, you are being presented to Her Majesty the Queen". This was the cue for Fredric to greet the Queen and share a sentence or two with the Royal Matriarch.

Later, Fredric jokingly said, "You could have told me she was the Queen, James, I couldn't see, after all."

Both James and Fredric stayed at my house that year during

the London Marathon.

I recall Fredric sitting in my living room, relaxing on the sofa, after their impressive marathon achievement.

I ran James a hot bath with some soothing oils and supplied him with a vast pint glass of strong gin and tonic, filled with ice and plenty of lemon. James was content relaxing in a hot bath and indulging in a well-deserved soak to soothe his aching muscles.

I poured Fredric a drink, and we settled into a chat. As I spoke to Fredric, he looked straight at me.

"Being blind allows me to see the person clearly. There are no distractions, just conversation and tone of voice."

Then he added, "I can see you, Vivika. As bright as day. I can understand why you and James get on like you do. It is my privilege to know you and be so welcome in your home."

Fredric and I conversed for a long time about all sorts. He was a pleasure to talk to.

Fredric gave me an insight that evening, which I have often reflected on. Even though he was a blind man, Fredric could see more than most."

Reliable Rock

When there was a reunion of Naval Officers at St James's Palace, James and his colleague and friend, Mike, came up to town.

"Very befitting to have your dinner at St James' Palace, King James," I laughed.

"Indeed, it is, my Queen. You too shall have access to enter your chariot, the spectacular Blossom Mobile".

With that, James gave me an A4-size white paper with a blue cross on it, rather like the Scottish flag. I think he called it the Lord Chamberlain cross, but I don't accurately recall.

"Here, Vivi," he said "this sign will allow you to enter anywhere and park wherever you want. It is valid for today."

I parked Blossom, bang in the middle of the courtyard of St James' Palace and delivered "my" officers, Immaculately groomed, and impeccably dressed in Black Tie.

At night, I picked them up from the same spot.

Slightly inebriated, they came out of St. James' Palace and shouted "Vivi, Blosh, we are coming."

Having whisked both James and Mike off home, they insisted

on climbing into my bed for a post-dinner chat. They were charming and cuddly, but not impertinent or inappropriate.

I then sent them off to sleep and tucked them up in bed, as they "insisted".

Next day, they were upbeat and charming. I loved their style. We showered and dressed and jumped back into Blossom. We set off for our traditional, heavily peppered, heavenly Bloody Mary's, to wash down our exquisite Eggs Benedict, at the Lanesborough Hotel. Afterwards, we crossed the road into Hyde Park for a stroll. We digested our food and the events from the night before.

Over time, I met up with James in different locations, with his cronies; Charles Woodston, Christian Hover, Edward Felix and the likes of "Sharpy", "Cunning" and "Spade".

We hooked up in Stockholm, Cyprus, Malta and other places. I got to know Woodston, Hover and Felix, as well as Mike, quite well. Wherever we went, and whenever we met, there was always magic and positivity.

I was deeply smitten with James and loved his whole being.

James made my soul sing. He made me feel safe and blissfully happy.

If ever I were in trouble of any sort, the first person I would call, was James.

One day, when I was driving in the Great Rift Valley in Jordan, on my way back from Aqaba to Amman, a business colleague and I were caught in a sandstorm. The result was that we couldn't see a thing. The road was closed, and the sand granules were coming in through the car's air conditioning, practically choking us.

On that occasion, all I could think about was CJ. He would

know what to do. He would know whom to call. I texted him from the Rift Valley. James was in Norway at the time.

He told me to dampen cloths and switch off the a/c. It is most essential to stop the dust from entering your lungs, he said via text message. Then he instructed me to send my location, so he could be sure of my exact whereabouts in case he needed to act .

It was a horrible and scary experience, but with CJ on stand-by, and knowing that he held power to send in help on the ground, I relaxed.

My colleague and I sat out the sandstorm and came out safely.

James not only inspired me, but he also challenged me to think. Whenever I had an issue, I would run it by him, and he would ask some questions. He would say or suggest a single thing that took my mind to another level. I loved that about him.

If ever we were planning to meet and James couldn't make it, I would naturally be disappointed.

He would say, "Vivi, I am not letting you down, I am letting you know."

A born diplomat, he was, "my" Captain James. To me, James was a superhero.

The kind of person who leaves a legacy and energy, long after they have gone."

After a short while, Lama, who was usually loud, now spoke quietly.

"Bless you, dearest Vivika, for sharing such precious memories in such vivid detail."

It was time to wrap up our call, which had been extraordinary for us all. Mostly for me, I felt, as I recalled events of all these years ago and the emotions they still stirred in me.

Check-in Shenanigans

"Albert, you made it!" I called out to Annie. Annie, hurtled towards me, knocking over the luggage of a fellow Gatwick traveller in her path.

"Sorry, mate," Annie yelled over her shoulder as she kept running, leaving the red-bearded man startled, in her wake.

"What do you mean, I made it? Of course, I made it, Albert. When have I ever let you down?" Annie said, laughing.

"Well, I have to say, you cut it rather fine," I teased her.

We hugged each other, locked arms, and set off towards Emirates Airlines' check-in.

"How have you been?" I asked with a smile. I was happy to see my friend.

Annie didn't answer, but instead suddenly shrieked and started to frantically look around her.

"My luggage. Where is my luggage?" Annie shouted.

"Oh bollocks, double damn and thrice damnation. What the bloody Nora was I thinking, or not thinking, I guess?" she ranted.

Annie realised she must have left her luggage on the Gatwick

Express on her journey down from London.

"Oh no," she scolded herself. "You have once again done it, royally well this time. You went and left your new bikinis on the train for some blooming tourist to pick up and take home."

And then added, "I blame you, Viv."

"Me?" I quipped incredulously while cracking up at Annie's far out and funny claim.

"Yup. You. You are the one who came up with this little adventure to "Dubious Dubai, Land of Sheets". It seems that our adventure has started very "sheet-ily" indeed. I must have been in such a deep state of pre-trip ecstasy. In the excitement, I left my gear on the train. This is very "sheet"!"

Annie stopped her outburst, and took a deep breath, trying to gain control. She closed her eyes, and exhaled three times with force. She composed herself.

"Now then," she spoke decisively.

"It is what it is. I will call "Lost and Found" once we have checked in. Nothing much we can do now. We have a holiday to go on."

With a broad grin, she turned to me, and said, "Shall we, Vic?"

I adored Annie, who was such an outrageous scatterbrain at times.

The fact that Annie jumped off the train and had not remembered to take her suitcase with her was no great surprise to me, nor, in fact, to Annie herself.

Annie was renowned for misplacing anything, from her exquisite rings to phones and from credit cards to the house and car keys. On this occasion, it was her luggage.

For someone so bright, creative, and capable, it was quite

extraordinary how absent-minded Annie could be.

"What are we going to do?" I said, turning to Annie with a look of concern.

"Vic, we are off to Dubai. I have been reliably informed that the shopping is fantastic there. So, if you don't mind me borrowing some of your clothes for tomorrow, I will shop endlessly for a new wardrobe. Now I have an excuse to shop till I drop if ever I needed one."

Annie laughed and helped me with my suitcase, as we made our way over to the check-in queue.

"Hang on a minute, angel," I said to Annie. "You're going towards the wrong queue."

"What are you talking about, dearest darling? This is Emirates. We are flying the UAE national airline if I am not mistaken?"

"We are, yes, but we need to change queues. The happy fact of the matter is that we will board the same plane, but we will be turning left."

"Turning left?"

A twinkle appeared in Annie's already bright and sparkling blue eyes.

"You mean "The Left Turn" that takes you into Business Class, rather than the right turn that takes you into Economy Class?"

"Yup, I pulled some strings and called in a favour from our well-placed friend in Emirates. Darling Jérôme managed to get us an upgrade".

"You, my girl, are simply awesome," Annie squealed.

"To be fair, we'll promote the airline to everyone we know. It is a great return on investment and the best thing Jérôme could have done for the airline." I said

"Classic class action, Vic. You are my forever heroine," Annie replied.

"Let's join the much shorter check-in queue for business. I love it!" Annie exclaimed.

"Albert, you too should get a useful job and build a strong travel network, like mine," I said to Annie.

"You need to start meeting new business contacts so you too can make a difference to the comfort of our travels. Much as you are talented, creative, and extraordinarily good at what you do, that does not get us business class seats. Not yet anyway. Maybe it will be different when you are a famous global award-winning film producer, but for now, my dear Albert, I guess we have to rely on me. It is because of me and my network that we can travel in the lap of luxury. For that, my dear, is where we belong," I said.

We joined the business class check-in queue. Then we suddenly stopped in our tracks. Annie, and I simultaneously inhaled more deeply. Then we looked at each other.

"Wow, what the hell is that?" I said.

"That fragrance. That heavy, intoxicating scent. How crazily delicious is that? Where is it coming from?" Annie asked.

"From the guys in front of us checking in, I think," I replied.

"I want to go and whiff them. The way they smell is even better than the way they look," Annie swooned.

"To be fair, I would not care about looks if a man smelt like that. It is a pure aphrodisiac. Even if he was not the most beautiful male, I think I would not be able to resist," Annie said.

The men in front of the line moved.

"Next please," the steward on the check-in desk called out

in his beautiful dulcet-toned voice.

We rolled my suitcase towards the check-in counter.

"Hello, ladies," the immaculately groomed airline check-in representative said.

"Please may I have your passports?"

I got mine out and said to Annie, "Passport, please Albert". Thank goodness Annie had kept it in the back pocket of her jeans, or else she would have been without a passport as well as without luggage.

The check-in steward, who was wearing a bright and shiny name tag that said, "Lee Loner", was now looking confused.

"Albert?" Lee Loner looked at Annie and said, "You don't look like an "Albert" to me." We both burst out laughing.

"People used to call us "V & A", for short. I am Vivika, and she is Annie."

"One day, Annie and I went to the Victoria and Albert Museum in London, in Kensington, the V&A.

That is when Annie and I, decided to adopt Queen Victoria and Prince Albert's names.

Annie calls me Vic or Queeny, and I call her Albert or Prince. V&A for short."

"I think V&A is more likely to mean "Ventures and Acquisitions," Lee laughed.

"I hope that those good-looking Arab men will show you what "Arab-style Investment" means. Let them put their funds in you. It can be very worthwhile. I speak from experience. My name may be "Lee Loner", but I am not a "Loner". I am a "Lover". And a great one too, or so I have been reliably informed. I am not just a pretty face."

Annie and I cracked up.

Lee then proceeded to check us in. Once he opened the relevant screen on the computer, he smiled coyly.

"Well, ladies," he said, "it is my pleasure to meet you. I see a note here from the magnificent Jérôme himself. I would die for that man. He is such a dish."

He briefly drew breath and went on, "I see here that you have been assigned the first row in business class. In the system, you are showing as both having birthdays.

However, I can see from your passports that this coincidental situation doesn't, in fact, reflect your birthdates. How odd," Lee beamed.

"Such a Jérôme thing to do. He is my eternal hero. Naturally, the system message from Big J. overrules anything that passports say. So, for me, today, even though I know better, you both have your birthdays. Congratulations, darlings. You don't look a day over twenty-one. What a great thing, to be travelling on this day when you first came to be. Ladies, that means oodles of champagne, with compliments from Emirates Airlines. You will be having quite a flight."

With an effeminate pout, Lee proceeded to tap something into the system. Then he was ready to check in the luggage. I placed my suitcase on the belt.

"Only one?" Lee inquired. "I have never seen two girls travel with only one suitcase."

"Don't ask," Annie laughed. "We will make up for lost luggage when we arrive in Dubai."

Lee proceeded to print out our boarding passes. He then tagged my luggage and sent it off down the belt. Finally, he folded his hands on the top of the desk and said,

"There, all done."

"Thank you so much, Lee," we said in unison.

"Amazing," I said. "You are a trooper of the first degree."

"No worries, girls," Lee said. "Just remember me to Jérôme. Tell him that Queen Lee says that, if Jérôme plays his cards right, he could be my Prince. He can then invite me to sit on his throne and let me take the best of care of his precious crown jewels."

Annie and I doubled up laughing.

Lee, encouraged by his responsive audience, was about to launch into another story. However, he didn't get the chance.

An Arab-looking man was moving towards the desk.

"*Khallas,*" the man barked. "Leave your flirting with these ladies for your home life.

Do your job. Check me in."

There was no "please", nor "thank you".

Annie and I suppressed a snigger. The irate man had no idea that Lee was not at all interested in women.

"*Au contraire*". He was responsive to this testosterone-infused alpha male.

"Certainly, Sir," Lee whispered in a smooth and seductive voice.

Lee did not appear upset at all. Instead, he seemed to be lapping it up and appeared to be ensconced in his next "check-in adventure". We said goodbye and whispered a heart-felt, "Thank you, Lee."

He acknowledged our gratitude with a professional look and bade us "a good trip".

He winked subtly, with a glint in his eye, and then immediately turned all his undivided attention to the irate passenger and started to handle "The heated Arab man".

"Jeez Louise," Annie said as we walked towards passport control, "did you smell that awesome scent again? I think it is an Arab aftershave and I can tell you that I love it."

"Yum," I said. "If they all smell that good, we may not even get around to shopping for your replacement wardrobe. We will be following these men like "bitches on heat"."

"Queeny, you crass moo. Can't believe you said that. Let's forget men. We need to get ourselves a suntan, some gorgeous garments made of pure silk, so they can hear our rustle as we arrive. Then we will indulge in some pearls and gold."

"Excellent plan, Acquisitions."

"Cheers, Ventures. Let's go and do some damage on the "cock-market", rather than the "stock-market"," Annie said.

Sniggering with hysterics, we successfully made it to the Emirates Business-Class Lounge where the bubble fest commenced and never stopped until we touched down in Dubai.

Lap of Luxury

Dubai, one of the seven United Arab Emirates, was only a seven-hour flight from London.

Not many people knew about Dubai in the late nineties, which is when Annie and I ventured out for a bit of a break.

From the moment Annie and I landed at Dubai International Airport, Annie could not stop going on about the "Men in Sheets".

It was not Annie's intent to insult or be disrespectful; it was merely her observant manner, and visual mind, that did the talking. Annie called a spade a spade, and a sheet, a sheet.

During our first trip to Jordan, there had hardly been any men in dish-dash.

However, in Dubai, most men wore the traditional Arab dress. "What do they wear under these sheets anyway?" Annie said. "We must find out while we are here. It could be valuable research for my next documentary," she laughed.

I had left the UK based airline, and was now working for an upscale international hotel chain. Ironically, in this job, I flew much more than in my previous one. The company managed hotels all over the world. I had many colleagues in the industry and, whenever we could, we would do each other favours.

I managed to get very competitive staff rates for our stay in Dubai.

My "rather more than good friend" Othman, had recently transferred to Dubai from Jordan, to become the number two in charge of this new hotel. I met him during sales calls in Europe. We became "close". I was infatuated with him.

"He is cheeky as sin and sexy as hell. He makes me melt. Whenever he looks at me in that way, or holds out his hand to me, I am his." I swooned, teasing Annie.

"Stop." Annie laughed. "What is this, an extract from *The Arabian Nights*?"

When I told Othman that Annie and I were coming to Dubai, he left no stone unturned. He upgraded our employee-rated booking, which would typically be for the lowest room category, to an exquisite suite. It featured a giant master bedroom and an additional twin-bedded room, which was more significant in size than most living rooms.

The bathroom boasted a sauna, a steam room and a Jacuzzi. The lush lounge area featured two massive sofas for at least twelve people each.

There were exotic-looking flowers everywhere. A massively oversized TV screen, placed on one of the walls in the main living room, gave access to endless movie options.

The kitchenette was more extensive than most people's kitchens at home.

There was heaps of space, tons of comfort and all the luxuries anyone could ever wish for.

Having settled in, the doorbell rang.

"That is odd," I said, "the luggage is already here".

It turned out that Othman had sent up a kilo of handmade chocolates, along with complimentary spa vouchers, a bottle of champagne and a selection of excursions for us to choose from. He treated us like queens.

"You have to admit, Annie, the guy has class," I laughed. "Got to say, he is a hell of a gentleman on the face of it,"

Annie agreed.

We placed the regal-looking box of chocolate treasures on the table in between the two twin beds in the second bedroom. We each got comfortable on our own queen bed and tucked into the chocolates.

"Fit for a King, or a Sultan, or a General," I said.

"I could get used to this," Annie said as she lay down on the bed, blowing kisses at the door. "Thank you, Othman. You have proved that you understand the female mind. The first thing any woman needs is chocolate. All else is secondary."

After a while, Annie said, "I think we need a workout."

"A workout, Annie?" I exclaimed, pretending to be horrified. "We are enjoying delicacies, and you suggest going to the gym?"

Annie held yet another chocolate between her long slender fingers. She fluttered her eyelashes a few times.

"There," she said, "that's better. That must have gotten rid of at least a quarter of a calorie."

"Now, what is our next choice, Vic?"

I spotted another chocolate I wanted, wedged it between my teeth and mumbled, "workout".

This time it was Annie's turn, to feign shock. Her eyes wide open, she gasped. "What?"

I closed my lips around another chocolate. Then bent and stretched both index fingers as a notional workout. Annie joined in. As we continued to chat and laugh, we polished off every one of them. Feeling a little sick after the indulgence, we simply lay down on the beds and chatted and laughed a lot. After an hour, Annie jumped off the bed.

"I am off for a run."

I decided to go for a coffee with Othman. He had looked after us so well and given us all our goodies and preferential treatment. I was up for a little tête à tête with him.

Having called down to check if he was free, I made my way to his office.

It was early evening, and most of the staff were out or had left for the day.

He closed the door, and switched on the "DND" sign, "Do Not Disturb".

"How are you and Annie settling in? Is there anything else I can do for you?" he said.

"You are awesome," I told him.

"We are in utter heaven. No one could have placed us more directly in the lap of luxury. Thank you for all the amazing gifts, attention, and kindness. Annie and I are overwhelmed and totally love everything you have arranged. Every detail is hugely appreciated. And as to your question, whether there is anything else that is needed, I only want one more thing, if it is not too much to ask," I flirted.

He did not hesitate.

Othman got up from behind his desk and came towards me. He put his arms around my waist and kissed me. Slowly, he started caressing me.

"I am missing our sales trips," he breathed. "We must plan some more missions and explore new markets," he mumbled. Then he kissed me more intensely. He hitched my dress up. "Hello, Puss," he said. "Long time no purr. Glad you came commando."

He smiled at me, his twinkling eyes expectant. He kissed me again, long, and lingering.

Then he went down on me.

With his expert tongue and capable hands, he prepared me for the delivery of his "pièce de résistance", which I could not, and did not, resist.

Right there on his desk, under the watchful eyes of the Emirati owner of the hotel, whose large photo was placed on the wall, he transported me to his Arab World.

Explosive and divine.

Later on, that evening, Annie, and I left the room to go for sushi in the hotel.

We made our way over to the glass lift, just as two men in Arabic dish-dash arrived.

They looked crisp, clean, and exotic. They smelt sensual and looked freshly groomed. *Attractive*, I thought.

Annie popped her hand into her small clutch bag. Seemingly accidentally, she dropped some dirham coins on the floor. Confused, I started to help her pick them up.

The men were watching us as we were scuttling around the bottom of their dish-dashes.

The scene was beyond bizarre. I could not help cracking up. The Arab men left. I could not blame them.

I said to Annie, "What the hell was that all about?"

She grinned. "I always wondered what they wear underneath their sheets. I thought if I dropped the change, we could legitimately scramble to try and peek."

Gut Feeling

Barbara Watts, who was a head-hunter in hospitality, called me. She asked whether I was available for a short-term role. Barbara explained a bit more. The Human Resources director of the organisation that had engaged her services needed someone to step in to cover the sales and marketing leadership role for six months.

When Barbara told me that Rory McLoughlin was the Managing Director of the hotel chain, I was sold.

Rory had been the rising star in my team when I worked for the airline when I first moved to the UK. At the time, I was his boss.

It struck me once again how small the global hospitality industry is. You work with people and lose touch and then, out of the blue, you are reconnected.

There is an industry rule that recommends you always leave on good terms from a job, as you never know when or where you may meet again.

Barbara went ahead and set up a meeting with Rory, who managed to fit me into his busy schedule. Barbara was delighted, and so was I. It would be great to see Rory again.

I made my way to the global headquarters, in the leafy suburbs of West London.

On arrival, I parked my car, entered the building, and went up to the lady at reception. I greeted her politely.

The receptionist smiled back at me. "Rory is waiting for you." She pointed to where he was standing. I turned around and looked up. He had been watching me from the balustrade on the mezzanine level.

He grinned at me and put his thumb up. "Come on up", he gestured.

I took the stairs to the first floor to greet him.

"Vivika, brilliant to see you." He embraced me warmly. "Do you still have "just a dash of milk" in your coffee?"

"Very impressive," I smiled. "Always said that cream rises. You are living proof."

He never interviewed me. We had coffee and caught up. The job was mine if I wanted it.

I started the following Monday and hit the ground running.

I had led sales and marketing teams before. This was a good company, with clear plans and "proper people" as I like to call them; decent, hard-working, fun-loving with "Can-Do, Will-Do" attitudes. They were a gorgeous bunch.

The initial six-month interim contract was extended to nine months. Time flew by.

I counted my blessings to be working with a great team and an inspired leader. Work was so much better if you had the right leadership in place. Rory was firm but fair. It was "All Good".

Towards the end of the contract, Rory asked me whether I would consider staying.

I thought about it but knew I had tackled the challenge and that the salary for a full-time job would be considerably less than I was getting on a contract basis.

We agreed I would stay until I got my next gig.

As luck would have it, I was approached by another recruitment professional.

The chap introduced himself as John Maynard. He sent me a message online.

It read, "Dear Ms Vivika, please forgive me for this unsolicited approach. I came across your profile. I think you are the perfect person for a role I have.

The position I am looking to fill is for a senior role in sales and general management, based in Central London."

I replied, asking which hotel chain was looking. John was quick to answer and emailed,

"What do you mean, which hotel group?" he answered. "This role has nothing to do with hotels or travel".

I was confused. I had only ever worked in hospitality. That was the only industry I was interested in. My experience was in hotels and airlines.

John went on.

"This is an extraordinary opportunity. Well paid. Leading a team in cosmetics.

Cosmetics?

Sure, I like to use it, but to sell it? What a soul-destroying thought. I knew myself reasonably well. I could never engage in something that did not interest me. Usually, I immediately dismissed something that did not resonate. My gut was saying "NO!".

However, as my interim role had pretty much ended, I decided to find out a little bit more about the potential opportunity. I called John Maynard on the number in his e-signature in the email.

Within thirty minutes of speaking to John, I received his message, saying, "Your interview is tomorrow at half-past two. The Cosmetic People look forward to meeting you at the Sheraton Hotel on Piccadilly".

I gave my mother a call and told her briefly about "the interview".

She sounded encouraged. I knew she always worried about my brother and me if we weren't "in a job" and she knew my interim role was ending.

We agreed to meet at Fortnum and Mason on Piccadilly at tea-time. That was equivalent to four o'clock in our family understanding.

I loved the iconic store, right in the middle of London.

I made a bit of an effort and applied some make-up for the interview. Dressed up for the occasion, I made my way to the meeting.

I arrived at the Sheraton Hotel.

It is a traditional property on Piccadilly, opposite Green Park. The art deco Palm Court is exquisite. Afternoon tea in this award-winning iconic space is something else. Typically, the harp is played by a talented musician. Against the backdrop of this art nouveau tea-room, exquisite tempting teasers, pastries and sandwiches are served. I loved listening to the sounds of Vivaldi's Four Seasons when I was younger. On occasions, my parents would take us to the theatre and for afternoon tea in

London. I loved it then, and I love it now.

On arrival, I was greeted by a "garçon", in grey.

"Good afternoon. We are expecting you, Ms Vivika," he said. I had not mentioned my name, but I could spot two eager-looking people beyond the reception desk, in the middle of the Palm Court.

Seated at a low table, they were motioning me to join them. Clearly, they had told the waiter my name and asked him to look out for me.

I smiled and made my way over to where they were sitting. When I reached them, I was introduced to the Director for Europe, Robert Sans and the Country Director of Germany, Helga Hauss.

"Good afternoon. How nice to meet you," Helga said, "We are so pleased to see you are wearing a dress."

"Excuse me?" I said. "Pleased that I am wearing a dress?" I repeated incredulously yet politely.

"Yes. We are a company zat deal wiz women. We want women in dresses to work wiz us."

Oh, my Lord. Get me out of here. What is this?

Then I remembered I was simply doing John a favour by going for this interview and decided to enjoy myself.

"Oh, absolutely," I said. "I can well imagine that wearing a dress is a clear sign of a professional approach, when working with women in the cosmetic industry. I cannot imagine anyone not presenting themselves at an interview in a robe."

Helga looked relieved.

"Exactly wot we sink." Helga's strong German accent was undeniable and somehow enhanced the funny side of "sings". Still smiling about Helga's pronunciation of the "th" as an "s", I said, "I would love to hear more about your company. Naturally, I have done my research." This was not true—a little white lie for the sake of it.

"I would like to learn from you about your aspirations and goals," I said, "then I can see whether I could contribute my talent, passion and energies to add value to your organisation."

I was taking the mickey now and entertaining myself. Robert relaxed. I was using the terms that aligned with his requirements. He was looking for clues to decide whether I could or could not do the job.

I was ticking all the boxes he was focusing on.

I decided to increase my level of entertainment. I peppered the conversations with buzz words that would no doubt resonate with Robert.

As I learnt more about the company, I was getting better at throwing "tick-box terms" in. I spoke about goals. I ticked that box. I moved on to "KPIs', Key Performance Indicators. Tick. I included a reference to "Women-Led-Organisation". Tick. Then I added a reference to "SWOT analysis', and took time to elaborate on strengths, weaknesses, opportunities and threats for good measure. Tick.

Tick-tock, all this ticking of subliminal boxes, made my brain wonder what time it was. I looked at my watch.

Time for tea and bubbly with my dearest Mama.

After a good fifty minutes, I thanked Helga and Robert for their time and told them that I had to be off.

I considered my job done. This role wasn't for me, of course, never would be.

Both Robert and Helga looked surprised.

"But we were not yet finished to ask you wot else we want to know. You are outstanding, and we wish you to remain and reveal more of yourself."

I suppressed a giggle. That came across as awkward, but Helga had no idea.

"Thank you, Helga, for your kind words, but I must, unfortunately, leave due to a previous commitment that I need to respect. Naturally, I can answer further questions at another time if that is relevant."

I picked up my bag, pashmina, and brolly, shook hands, smiled warmly, straightened out my dress and left.

I crossed the road towards Green Park and turned left down Piccadilly in the direction of Fortnum and Mason.

My mother had just arrived when I came in. We hugged each other and sat down.

We settled into conversation and scones.

I regaled my mother with the hilarious story of how John had asked me to attend the interview and how it had gone.

My mother enjoyed the anecdotes and at the same time said, "It's amusing, Viv darling, I can see that, and yes, I had to laugh."

Then she paused just a little bit too long for comfort and continued, "But it will not be a laughing matter when you are out of a job. You cannot be "in-between" jobs for too long. And maybe it is better to have a bird in the hand."

"Mummy, I know. Don't worry, I will land something soon. The meeting I went to just now was not a real job interview, but it was worth the effort to share the story and do this guy John a favour." I left it at that.

We continued with our selection of exquisite smoked

salmon and cucumber sandwiches, little gourmet creations, with exciting flavours. We started with our favourite Fortnum and Mason's Darjeeling tea, followed by a couple of glasses of Champagne. We enjoyed a great afternoon, chatting about the new neighbours who had just moved in next door, the state of the garden, the repainted summer house and my mother's research in the British Library, amongst other things.

"Do come for Sunday lunch soon, Viv," my mother said. "Daddy is not getting any younger. I am increasingly concerned with his ability to remember things. I am not saying it is Alzheimer's, but sometimes, I wonder."

"Don't worry, Mummy, I am coming down, this week or the next," I said.

I vowed I would be.

What my mother said about my dad, pulled me up short.

My parents would not be around forever. I swallowed hard and moved my mind on from thinking about the unavoidable.

I thought about my parents' relationship. They were very different people.

They now lived in England, where my mother was originally from. My father was Dutch. We grew up in the Netherlands. Every so often, my parents would go to England to visit my grandmother. They usually stayed at "The Cottage". This Victorian three-bedroomed house, which was charming and homely, belonged to my lovely aunt and uncle, the most generous and interesting people you could hope to meet. Growing up, we spent most of our holidays there.

My mother loved being outdoors. Building massive bonfires and getting stuck into the garden was her thing. After an early morning walk across the fields, dear Mama would embrace the day. With the dew still on the lavender and the ducks on the massive pond, my mother would drink her coffee. Perched against the brick wall, taking in the fresh air and natural surroundings, she would simply breathe. An expression of entire satisfaction was discernible, not only from her face but from her whole posture.

If I happened to wake up early, I found her in her jeans or joggers. She smiled at me so happily.

"Good morning, darling," she would say, with a tone of joy in her voice.

"Good morning," I would grunt, sounding like a genuinely stroppy, unsatisfied, and ungrateful pubescent individual, which I was.

I was not a charming teenager, I must be honest. I was what you might describe as "hard work".

If the weather were good, my mum would bring out a chair from the living room and soak up the rays. She loved the sun on her face. But even in the rain, she was happy to be out.

We'd hear the latch on the back door as she came back from a long walk. Having kicked off her Wellington boots, she'd go through to the living room.

Licking her lips and smiling, she readjusted her dark, short, curly hair.

With a healthy glow on her rosy cheeks, she looked at us with an expression of deep satisfaction, utterly refreshed, and said, "Time for tea. Vivi, be a love and pop the kettle on. Martin, darling, please be the strong man that you are and fetch a basket of logs from the shed. I will then fix the fire".

After a break of tea, biscuits and chat, my mother would continue her morning activities. She would get stuck into some serious weeding, trimming, and pruning.

The soil and the fresh air made her feel alive. The positive energy of the land lifted her spirits and made her happy and at peace.

When I moved to the UK, it was a joy to see my parents in The Cottage. I'd drive down from London to spend the weekend with them.

At that time, I was no longer a recalcitrant teenager, and I looked forward to joining her on her morning walks and appreciated these times with my mum, stomping across the glorious countryside.

One day, a tree had come down and fallen into the muddy pond. In her red trousers and signature cream and blue Breton top, my mum decided to "go in". She fixed a rope around her middle and tied the other end to one of the healthy trees next to the "lake".

The pond was perhaps not a good description as it was more like a mini lake.

My mother waded into the water. Although she had taken the precaution of securing herself to the tree, it was risky.

On that weekend, I was down from London with my toy-boy Ben, whom my mother loved. Ben was practical and enjoyed the great outdoors too. He was happy to assist my mum in her mission.

To haul the tree out of the pond, we tied it to my car, Blossom. With the roof down, I drove. Ben pulled from the back seat of the Beetle, and my mum pushed from her spot in the lake.

Through teamwork, we managed to extract the fallen tree from the lake.

We naturally congratulated ourselves on a "job well done". After our hard work, Ben whipped up his signature creamy scrambled eggs with bacon, accompanied by fresh grapefruit juice.

I have a picture of my mum on that day. The happiness that radiates from that photo is incredible. My mother recognised what made her soul sing.

She put up with what was needed. She sacrificed a lot, yet never complained.

Strength and compassion are the hallmarks I most associate with my much-loved mother.

I inherited my mother's DNA in terms of loving life and pursuing adventure.

We both clearly know what makes us tick, though my mum is a much kinder, more patient and accommodating person than I could ever hope to be.

Whenever my parents were in the UK, my father would check the listings of properties that were for sale. Occasionally, he went to see a house that was on the market.

No viewing ever led to anything more, but it was fair to say that my mother's hopes were building.

"A future home in England may well be on the cards, Vivi," she once said to me over a cup of tea, with a glimmer of hope in her loving eyes.

My parents were out on an evening walk with friends in Kent when they spotted a lovely house.

My parents' friends said that this enclave enjoyed the most spectacular views from the back gardens. Later on, that afternoon, my mother was speaking animatedly about the possibility of moving to England after retirement. My father said how much he liked the house too. When my mother asked whether they should put in an offer and consider moving to the UK from Holland, my dad was slightly shocked and said,

"Move to England? I was not thinking about that at all."

"But" my mother stammered, "we went to look at this house and we both loved it, yet you have no interest? You were only just looking for the sake of looking with no intentions whatso-ever?" My mother was distraught. She genuinely thought that my dad had been serious this time.

I spoke with my mother on the telephone. She sounded sad and depressed.

After this conversation with my mum, I called my dad and explained how my mother was feeling. I think the penny dropped. Something changed in him.

Surprisingly and fantastically, he called me the next day and said, "I think I will put in an offer on the house".

I was so happy. My mother was overjoyed. The house was bought.

A new adventure and era were about to open up.

Caveat Card

I woke up later than usual to the sound of my mobile phone ringing. John's number appeared.

"Hi, John, good morning," I said.

"Good morning, Vivika. Well, I wanted to debrief you on your meeting with the cosmetics company yesterday."

"It was a big day for you, John. All three of your candidates were seen yesterday. The banker, the nutritionists and me. I think I was the last of the day, wasn't I?"

"Yes," he said. "All three of you were interviewed. You may have been the last of the day, but you are their top choice."

"What? What do you mean?" I said.

"They simply loved you," John said. "They thought you were refreshing and different. Helga said you understood her very well. And that you wore a dress."

I was utterly speechless, which is a rare occurrence. Then I got the giggles.

"John," I said, "As you know, I was doing you a favour, and that was my great pleasure, but this is ridiculous. No way have I any interest in this position whatsoever, even if I am not going to have a job."

"That is the very point, dear Vivika. The very point. You don't have a job. They loved you. You just did not love them back. But you may do in time if you try."

"No, John, that wasn't the deal."

"I know," he said, "but think about it. You could have a well-paid senior leadership role and strengthen your c.v., all the while earning good money and travelling too. What do you have to lose?"

"Are you suggesting I keep going with this?"

"Yes. Name your price and let us see how far you can get."

John was charming and determined, clearly keen on landing a hefty commission check.

I remembered what my mum said, "You can't be "in-between" for too long, darling".

Then I thought about what she said about my dad. I did not want to be that burden to my dear mum. She was stretched enough, and I loved her deeply and respected her for all she had given up for all of us. She could do without the strain and worry on my behalf.

So, I said to John, "OK, if they want to see me again, I will do it."

"Really?" He was clearly delighted and verging on the ecstatic. "I will call them and let them know."

"John," I said, "I will continue on the journey. However, I can tell you from now that my requested salary will be high. Do you know what they are offering?"

"It is a six-figure salary," John said.

"I know, John, but there are many figures between 100K and 999K which are equally six-figure numbers, so let's see how much we can get them to budge."

I had to put in the caveat of the salary. I needed an opt-out card to play for this job that I, in my heart of hearts, did not want. Naming an exorbitant salary would elegantly solve that issue.

Over the following weeks, matters got silly. I had six more interviews and then did a test.

I spoke with the head offices in Canada and Ukraine and then met the head honcho in London, who had flown in to meet me.

Then, the day came when John delivered the "good news."

"They want you." John was triumphant. "Imagine, you made it through. Congratulations. This is terrific news." He sounded beside himself with joy.

I, on the other hand, felt my heart sink. I knew this was not for me. I was also acutely aware that I needed a job. Another part of me did not want my mother to worry unduly.

I recalled the conversation with Rory McLoughlin.

During the interim role, he said that it may well be an idea to gain some experience outside the hospitality industry. By doing so, I could build versatility and resilience.

Rory was planning to do just that.

I thought about what Rory had said. Nothing ventured, nothing gained. Perhaps I was just too judgmental and rigid. After all, I always advocated adventure. Still not convinced, I decided to push back one more time. If, after that, it was still on the cards, it was indeed meant to be.

Playing my caveat card with John, I said, "Wow, unbelievable John, I am amazed," and I honestly was, "but we have not yet settled on the salary."

John was quiet and then said, "I thought we discussed the salary level."

"You said a six-figure salary, not the amount."

"OK," he said, hesitantly, "what is your price?"

"Anything over a hundred and sixty thousand British pounds per annum," I said without hesitation.

That would do it. I would be turned down. Then I could have a valid reason, saying that the Cosmetics Group did not offer me the job, which would be the truth, albeit a sculpted one.

John uttered, "Vivika, this is more than half again over the salary level that I am expecting."

"If they accept, then I will give it my best and do the job," I said.

"So, if I get an agreement on the financial package, you will accept?" he asked.

"Yes, I will."

That would never happen...

Relieved, I hung up.

Imagine. Cosmetics. Working with so many women. All of them synching in their menstrual cycles. And all of them into make-up. This was most definitely not my scene.

Not My Thing

I was enjoying a coffee on my gorgeous and perfectly formed lush patio, where I was soaking up the sunshine at 11.11 in the morning. My favourite time. Usually.

Sitting pretty in the sunshine, in nothing more than my yellow primrose towel, my phone rang, I answered. It was John.

"Hey, John, morning. How are you?"

"All is more than excellent," he replied.

Without stopping for breath, he continued,

"They have accepted your demands. They want you to start next week. The team has been without a leader for too long, so boom," he added, "you pitched your price at a time when they liked you very much. They more than need you. They have accepted your terms. We have a go."

Oh No. I felt sick. *Seriously? Could this be happening?*

I didn't know what to say. I had played the caveat card, had bluffed, and lost.

Naturally, John thought we had both won. "Vivika," he said, "are you there?"

"Yes," I stumbled, "I am here."

"I can quite imagine you must be utterly speechless. It is a hefty offer, which you are now able to say yes to".

Clearly relieved, he sighed. "I guess we can proceed, my dear, as we have overcome all the barriers. Congratulations. Can I confirm your start-date next week?"

My mind was racing, but fair was fair. And nothing was forever. "Yes, John, go ahead." What else could I have reasonably said?

"Good stuff. Let me get this doggy washed." Then he rang off.

Get this doggy washed? The expression was random. I doubted it existed, yet it somehow effectively described the prolonged process we had gone through.

After John hung up, I found myself laughing helplessly at this ridiculous reality, which was born out of "doing John a favour". I didn't call my mum for two days after I received the "good" news.

When the contract arrived a few days later, I tried to find things at fault in the papers, to look for a reasonable way out, but couldn't. I resigned myself to signing what was needed, promising myself an opt-out.

I made a mental pact with myself. If, after eight months, I hated the job, I would leave.

The journey that followed was something I could not have envisaged or rationally imagined. The company, for the most part, employed women only.

The ladies were professional and committed. Top sales-women received endless awards and graduated through the career tiers. It was akin to calling people by their rank in the armed forces, but then in a cosmetic sales context.

Apart from the ladies, this job was not for me. "Cosmetics" was not my thing. I had ended up in a parallel world that did not resonate in any way, shape or form.

After eight months of being in the job, I flew to the Head Office in Canada. I felt I was on an endless treadmill of bizarreness. I did not fit in. Whatever I did seemed alien and out of context. I had never had the feeling of being lost when I worked in the airline or hotels.

I knew what "good" felt like. And this was not it.

I popped into the bookshop at the airport to pick up a novel and some magazines. I was trying to find a way to kill some time on the long-haul flight.

A little book caught my eye. It was concise. Much smaller than the other covers. It was black with red and green writing on it. I took a closer look. It was called, "The Question Book; What Makes You Tick?", by Mikael Krogerus and Roman Tschappeler. I should perhaps ask myself some of these critical questions, to find out what I wanted out of life. The one I was living was definitely not the one I wanted.

I completed the questions during my flight.

On re-reading the answers, it starkly revealed how I felt at that time. A few randomly selected questions painted a vivid picture. One of the questions asked, "What is something you forgot?" My answer - "That life is excellent."

Next question: "Was this your best year so far?"

The answer, "Definitely not. My worst, probably". Next question, "Why?"

The answer, "Lack of purpose, the wrong job, no time to

meet up with My Posse, no energy or sense of direction".

I looked back down at "The Little Book of Questions", which lay open in my lap.

Question: "Do you think you act your age?" My answer was, "Yes, I am ageless".

Question: "What is the most overrated virtue, in your opinion?" The answer: "The concern around "reputation" and what other people think of you, versus "identity", meaning who you are and what you stand for and what you believe in."

In my experience, multiple factors have to add up, not just the money. And nothing was adding up, so I decided to take a leap of faith. My inner wisdom egged me on. *If you don't jump, you will never land on your feet.*

I was clear. When in Canada, I did what was needed and then handed in my notice.

That was the end of my job and my six-figure pay check.

But it was the start of going back to being me.

I was excited at the prospect.

Lift Off

The annual travel trade fair was due to take place in Dubai the following week. I booked my flight and made arrangements.

I spent four days and three nights in Dubai. I met former colleagues and old friends.

Slowly but surely, I felt my lifeblood coursing through my veins again. I was back on my patch.

I managed to meet a significant number of hotel contacts, and there were a few opportunities that I decided to apply for.

Because I knew the players in the market, it did not take long. I landed a job on day two of the fair. It was going to be in Abu Dhabi, not a place I knew, but it was just an hour drive away from Dubai.

I would go back to the UK and say my goodbyes and clean up my "lock and leave" pad. After that, I would catch the flight from London to Abu Dhabi. I was going to lead the sales and marketing department for one of the luxury city hotels in the capital of the UAE.

I was back in hospitality—what a relief.

The travel industry is a People Business.

It attracts professionals interested in moving around. This sector appeals to those who enjoy working in different places and to those who get energy from other humans, from new places and novel experiences.

Romance and promiscuity seem to come with the package. Travel industry professionals have a reputation of hooking up with total strangers, clients, and colleagues, wherever they may be in the world.

After a little line up of B52 shots, off they hurtle into the reaches of anyone's open arms, straight into bed.

It appears to be the same for both men and women, in equal measure.

Travel trade-fairs around the globe are rampant sex affairs. Adultery. Threesomes. Orgies. You name it. If you want it, you can have it—all in the name of connecting continents and exchanging experiences.

People who work for rival companies during the day, or "the competitive set", fraternise and fuse at night.

The next day, when the lust-fest is over, those same individuals, go back to being foes.

Pilots have a reputation for being the "Kings of Promiscuity".

With them, all sorts of shenanigans go down; go down, as in "Cunni Lingus", as opposed to "Aer Lingus".

I can tell you from experience.

I knew a pilot, Karim. He used to fly for the leading Middle Eastern Airline.

I met him online. He was based in Dubai but, naturally, did not spend much time there as he flew around the world.

We chatted frequently. That is the beauty of online. We

could always connect, and we often did.

When Karim heard I was in Dubai, where he happened to be too at the time, he came to see me at the hotel.

I was staying at my favourite property, on Dubai Creek.

I gave him a call, letting him know I was in town.

"Perfect," Karim said when he knew my whereabouts.

"I need to fly tomorrow. You are only ten minutes from the airport. Give me an hour. I will be with you at around nine o'clock."

"I will give you an hour," I flirted.

Karim told me, "I will want a lot more than an hour with you, Vivika. Especially since it will be the very first time we meet in the flesh. Now let me get ready. Can't wait to meet you in person."

Karim was half-Moroccan, half-German and definitely a "Sexy Mudda Fucka", as Hélène would say. I always associated that expression with her.

He was dark-haired in a blond sort of way. He was a broader, taller, more European version of an Arab man.

We laughed on meeting each other for the first time, after all our online conversations. We chatted easily over a bottle of wine or two.

He spoke French, Arabic, German, English and Japanese. "Quite the linguist," I said.

"*Jawohl, akeed*, for sure, permit me to prove it to you."

He took me over to the wide windowsill and laid me down. The roller blinds were up, allowing for a spectacular view over Dubai Creek.

"I like to leave the lights on," he said, "so I can see what I am eating".

He took a pillow off the bed and popped it under my head. "*Alors, ma chérie*, are you lying comfortably?" he said in a French accent.

"Very comfortably, *merci*," I answered.

"*Parfait*," he smiled.

Karim proceeded to perform the most exquisite linguistic tongue twisters a girl could wish for. After that night, I called him "The Linguist". He could pleasure any woman in any language, with his skilful tongue and his charismatic way.

Karim stayed the night. He was due to fly out of Dubai to Paris in the morning.

I asked, "What if you still have alcohol in your blood when you are due to fly?"

"I hope my co-pilot did not drink. In the current circumstances, I will have to rely on him to take the controls. But don't worry," he said, "there is always auto-pilot to back us up if neither of us is in a fit state to fly the plane."

He grinned, jumped under the shower, slipped his clothes on, kissed me farewell and went off to fly an Airbus-380 to Paris.

Priscilla

Having moved from London to Abu Dhabi, the first real friend I made was Priscilla.

She was Australian and had moved to the UAE about six months before I did.

Priscilla, or Priss, as I called her, was the youngest high-flying director at a large international marketing firm, with its Middle East regional HQ in Abu Dhabi.

Her office was next to the hotel where I worked.

She used to have her nails and sugaring done by Sura, the resident owner of the salon in the hotel.

Sugaring was the Arabian alternative for waxing. I referred to having the hair removed "down under" as "sugaring puss", which became an adopted term within The Pussy Posse.

One day, I was having my hair done when Priscilla walked in. She asked for an eyebrow tattoo, which, at that time, was a new trend. The beauticians, mostly from the Philippines, giggled and said they didn't offer tattoos apart from the Henna ones.

Priscilla, said "Henna tattoos? What are they?" Sura jumped into the conversation and explained.

"Ms Priscilla, in the Arab world, women often apply henna for fun, but some still do it for magical reasons, to protect them against witchcraft or "the evil eye"."

I was intrigued as I overheard the conversation and asked Dr Google about the roots of Henna tattoos. I read, "Many designs are there to ward off evil. For over five thousand years, henna has been a symbol of good luck, health and sensuality in the Arab world. Arab brides still have henna parties with their girlfriends before the wedding. It carries good luck and fertility".

"Oh Lordy," Priscilla said, "I am so glad I asked you for eyebrow tattoos, otherwise, I would never have known about this great tradition. I will come back as soon as my Arab boyfriend asks me to marry him. Not that I am convinced about tying the knot.

It seems that his mother is the only woman who counts. I do know that the Arabian mother is the ultimate, pivotal person in the family. I am not planning on being "the lesser woman" and playing second fiddle to his mum, no matter how attractive my "Man in White" is."

There were more giggles from the staff. I was intrigued.

This girl was clearly Australian, and not from the UAE, but seemed to be exploring some significant local routes, including dating a UAE national, by the sounds of it.

Interesting, I thought. *What would it be like to have a relationship with someone born and raised in the Emirates? How would be to be in a long-term relationship with an Arab man?*

"I will definitely come back for a henna design. But for now, let me get a turquoise and tangerine mani". Then turning to me, Priscilla smiled and said,

"Hi, aren't you in charge of the sales peeps here at the hotel? We haven't met, but I have seen you around. Your guys and girls are always coming into my office, touting for our business. Where else would we go when you are right next door?" she laughed.

My hair was done, and I was due to go back to the office. But for some reason, I was drawn to this positive spirit of a girl and stayed for a manicure. We sat there for an hour, in big white leather seats, next to each other, yapping away.

From that day onwards Priss and I met up for lunch and hung out together. She was a joy to be with.

Her Arab Beau, a wealthy Emirati, was a high-ranking army official, but by the sound of it, also very much a "Mummy's Boy". *Weird*, I thought. The two didn't seem to equate. However, I later learned that most Arab men seem to crumble and swoon in the presence of their mothers. Mothers are adored, respected, and idolised.

Don't get me wrong, my mother means the world to me, but she would never choose to be the ruling Matriarch of my life. She is my friend and my confidante, but not the person who makes my life decisions.

An Arab man, however, seemingly will do as his mama says. Especially as it relates to matrimony. Arranged marriages in the Middle East are commonplace. The focus is on keeping the wealth and the reputation of the family intact. Love is a notion that is the least of their concern, or so it appears to the untrained European heart and mind.

One day towards the end of December, Priscilla arrived at my office.

"Hey, girl," I greeted her. "What an unexpected pleasure; come in. Coffee?" I said.

"It will have to be something stiffer. I broke up with Z last night. He told me he got engaged to his first cousin, who had been promised to him from birth. He said his mother had insisted and he could not refuse anything his mother requested from him. Z said that he loved me and always wanted me by his side, even if he could not marry me and for me to be his first wife. I must have looked flabbergasted. Z went on to tell me that over time, I could be his second wife since he was legally allowed to have four at one time."

"Oh," my dear Lord, poor you, Priss. What an utter swine. How could he do such a thing?"

I had never heard of anyone marrying their cousin or being freshly engaged and suggesting a continuation of the other relationship. It was disturbing and mind-blowing.

"Hey, you know what?" Priscilla continued, "I was so shocked I didn't know what emotion would come out. First, I got angry. Then I broke down and cried. Now, I somehow feel relieved that I am not on a slippery slope to sadness."

No sooner had Priscilla spoken about her logical response, than she welled up. I passed her a cup of coffee and gave her a hug. Then Priss chuckled through her tears.

"What's funny?" I asked.

"Well, to be honest, Viv, who wants to marry a man in a dress?"

"Quite right," I said. "Time to move away from a "sheet-y scenario". Best to get this chapter closed and be ready for a bright new year ahead. Let us do drinks tonight at "Diamonds and Pearls" and set the world to rights over a bottle of bubbly."

And that is what we did. We let the sun set and raised our glasses.

"Shits will be shits, and sheets will be sheets. Onwards and upwards," we toasted.

Annie, Hélène and I agreed to spend New Year together in Abu Dhabi.

Hélène was planning to fly in from Amsterdam and Annie from London.

They were both due to arrive on the 30th of December and planned to stay for a long weekend.

I asked the girls if they were OK to have Priscilla join us, which they were.

We kicked off our celebrations on my balcony and indulged in delicious tapas and pink champagne. We did not see the need to wait until midnight to pop the cork on the bubbles.

We all agreed that Priss should join The Pussy Posse. She fitted right in.

At midnight, we raised a toast to both the new year and to our freshly welcomed inner-circle confidante.

"To you and all who sail in you, Priss," I toasted.

Then, Annie, Hélène and I shared our sisterhood vow with Priscilla.

"Through thick and thin. And through sick and sin". Priscilla repeated the vow. We once again toasted, sipped from our replenished glasses, and hugged. Priscilla was now part of our sisterhood.

From then on, we officially flew in a formation of four.

Charming Company

The owner of the hotel where I worked was an Emirati named Ali.

He was handsome, competent, and utterly confident in every way. Or so it seemed.

Ali typically arrived at his city property in Abu Dhabi, in one of his many exquisite cars. He was always pristinely dressed in his snow-white dish-dash.

In Saudi Arabia, they call it a thobe. In the UAE and Oman, they call it a kandura.

I personally called it a dish-dash, as they did in Jordan. Annie referred to the traditional Arab dress as "a sheet".

Ali always wore his signature scent, which announced his arrival.

I was intrigued by Ali, from the minute I laid eyes on him. Well-bred and well-educated, he exuded undeniable elegance and class.

Under the leadership of Ali's late father, the family constructed an opulent hotel in the Eastern Desert, very near the Saudi border. The construction of this grand resort property was entirely strategic. Underneath, there was a significant oil reserve. They built the hotel on top of the well to ensure the black gold was protected from exploitation by the Saudi's. Hence, the property functioned as security. If ever the family decided to exploit the oil, the hotel would have to be destroyed. Even though the original construction cost of the property ran into the hundreds of millions of dollars, it would only take days to regain that money, once an exploration of the oil commenced. The Oasis Resort attracted both wealthy Europeans and Arabs, seeking escape in the depth of the desert. Luxurious, yet discreet, it appealed to royalty, the wealthy and the famous, seeking a place to play in private, away from prying eyes, in opulence and decadence.

The Oasis Resort was a playground for the "Über Rich".

When, quite suddenly, Ali's father, who was one of the most well-known and prominent businessmen in the UAE, passed away, Ali was fast-tracked into taking on specific parts of the family business. Ali was made responsible for all the hotels, including the one where I worked in the city.

Ali came to "my" hotel regularly. He would either work from "the Owner's Office", or sit in the lobby of the hotel, where more tended to be going on, which he seemed to prefer. He would always have several people around him. I was never quite sure who they were, or what they did.

On one occasion, when Ali was having coffee with his friends in the seating area next to the reception desk, I was talking to the front office manager.

Ali caught my attention and asked me if I had a phone charger. "Naturally, Mr Ali," I said and went to get the device and plugged it in next to where he was sitting. I noticed he watched me bending over, making me suddenly aware of my bum, not too far from his handsome face. "Thank you, Ms Vivika," he said.

"My pleasure, Mr Ali," I replied, noting that he remembered my name.

I smiled politely and left him to it.

Later on, that very same day, I bumped into Ali a second time. "Hello," he said, "didn't you know? It is my birthday. As the owner of this hotel, I would have expected you to wish me a happy birthday at least."

He gave me a cheeky grin. *Little flirt*, I thought, but it made me smile.

"I am so sorry, Sir," I said, "I was only just made aware."

He winked at me. He looked incredibly handsome in his designer attire, that hid, yet, at the same time, alluded to his perfect physique.

"Well, I expect a bit more from you on my birthday than just an excuse of not knowing."

I smiled and said, "I beg your pardon, Mr Ali. I must go, I have a hotel to sell."

He laughed and, in his most British manner, replied, "I bid you a good afternoon, Ms Vivika. May you do some good deals, and there is never any need to beg me."

He winked again and looked at me with his head slightly tilted, and a lazy smile.

I made my way to my office. Never had he been so familiar with me.

I admit I was taken by surprise, though was also amused.

Cheeky young buck, I thought. *Wherever you go, men will indulge in a little flirting, if they possibly can. Boys will be boys.*

I made my way to the hotel patisserie and spoke to Philippe, the pastry chef. I explained it was Mr Ali's birthday. We selected the most exquisite chocolate cake and wrote "Happy Birthday" in liquid chocolate on it.

Philippe agreed to box up the cake and keep it cooled until such time as Mr Ali was due to leave.

I nipped back to the sales office. I had a stash of cards for special occasions, which I kept in the bottom drawer of my desk. I selected an oversized, large square card made of heavy cream paper, with a giant bright orange balloon on it. Everyone who was in the office at the time added a birthday message. I dropped the card off at Philippe's office.

When Mr Ali left the hotel, the concierge placed the cake securely onto the passenger seat of the Mercedes G-wagon.

Ali was around twelve years my junior. Though he was the big boss, I knew that little things could make the difference, whether you were young or old, rich or poor, or whether you were the boss or not.

Indulging Ali on his birthday with an unexpected gesture would likely make him smile. I liked little impromptu initiatives that brought good energy.

That evening, I received a message from a number I did not recognise. It was Ali.

"Dear Ms Vivika", he wrote. "Thank you for your very rich, and chocolaty attention. It was much appreciated. I will have to find a satisfying way to work off the calories. If you have any ideas as to how, please let me know.

With my warmest thanks, Ali K".

Cheeky bugger, I smiled. *Or more precisely, cheeky handsome bugger. Ali knows full well he is charming, fit and all of that.*

But I will not let him treat me like a Cougar. Let me give him something to contemplate.

In the Middle East, men take flirting to new heights. Their aim is not to hunt for wives, but for conquests. It is the nature of the beast—the thrill of the kill.

I was ready to play ball.

Game on, I decided. I wrote back.

"Dear Mr Ali, I am glad you were able to indulge. I know you will be back to your disciplined self after your celebration. Any temptation you may have given into today will be but a memory tomorrow. Best, Vivika"

I smiled. *There you go. Take that, you yummy boy.*

A reply message from Ali. I felt a strange excitement.

It read, "Hello, Ms Vivika, I have some matters to discuss with you. I would like to do so over lunch tomorrow, away from your workplace".

Weird. But on a roll, I responded.

"Certainly, Sir, that fits with my schedule. Do please let me know where and when. I have a three o'clock. I must be back on at the hotel at that time."

It was a lie. I didn't have any afternoon appointments to rush back for. I would be darned if I would let Ali know that he could have my entire day if he wanted it.

He replied, "La Bella. One o'clock".

I knew that was one of "the other" properties, which the family owned.

I waited for twenty minutes before I replied and simply wrote, "Confirmed".

La Bella featured a great restaurant, serving an exciting mix of Lebanese and Italian. Pizzas with "Levant-inspired" mezze on top were my idea of heaven. It was quite a glorious and original combination. The chef at La Bella pushed culinary limits to new heights. An invitation for lunch at La Bella was a welcome prospect.

The hotel driver dropped me off. I made my way up to the concierge, who said,

"Ah, Ms Vivika, we have been expecting you. Lunch has been laid for you and Mr Ali in one of our get-away villas."

Oh, my goodness. I recalled the words "ideal for a romantic get-away," in their recent advertising campaign.

I was escorted to the villa, where Mr Ali was waiting for me with his driver, whom he instructed to leave.

He smiled at me and said, "Thank you for coming to meet me, Ms Vivika. I wanted to get to know you better and did not want to be disturbed."

Get to know me better?

I was confused and slightly thrown but did not let on. I thought this was going to be purely a business meeting, but from Ali's body language and words, that did not appear to be his intention.

What did he want?

I composed myself and decided to find out what he was planning to discuss.

"Please, Ms Vivika," he said. "Take a seat."

He invited me to settle on the comfortable sofa in the lush patio setting.

"Or would you prefer to go inside?" he asked, charm personified.

"Outside is perfect," I said, in my most confident manner.

Going inside the villa, just him and me, somehow seemed slightly suggestive.

I was feeling a bit discombobulated and thrown. Ali noticed and smiled.

"Don't worry, Ms Vivika. You are in charge here. I just want to explore opportunities."

"*Opportunities?*"

Ali made it sound like he was setting me up for an encounter that would involve more than just business.

Presumptuous, to say the least. Ali was walking a thin line.

I decided to enjoy his antics. Two can play at that game. I composed myself, ready for any eventuality that may come my way.

"I took the liberty of ordering some sashimi of salmon and tuna," Ali said.

"Do you like it hot?"

"No," I said, "Just average is what works for me."

I was rising to my game now, warming up for verbal battle.

I liked the challenge. And he clearly was one.

"Really?" Ali was clearly enjoying the banter. "Somehow, I don't quite believe that Ms V."

"Well, that is how it is. Pretty even keel, me. I don't like it spicy." I smiled.

"Nothing too exotic or exciting. Predictable and dependable, that is me."

He tilted his head, just like he had the day before at the hotel. His beautiful dark eyes twinkled, deep and tribal, yet cheeky and sophisticated.

"I am not so sure about that," Ali said, "I am not so sure about that at all."

Damn, how to respond to that?

If we were playing a game of tennis, the score would be fifteen-love to the young millionaire. Or perhaps it was a "straight ace".

Well, this game, set and match were not going to be won by Ali, I decided.

Ali interrupted my thoughts.

"What can I get you? Would you like a glass of wine?"

"No, thank you," I responded.

I thought he probably didn't drink. I was about to have lunch with the owner, who was twelve years my junior. He was flirting with me. It felt like I could be playing with fire if I started having a vino at this time of day.

With great resolve, as I must admit I loved a glass of wine at lunch, I said,

"Please can I have a glass of sparkling water, with a lot of ice and lemon?"

"We shall get you a cold glass of bubbling mineral water, to help you cool off."

Ali paused and looked at me, intently.

"You appear to be flustered, and I suspect, quite hot."

I blushed. I don't know whether Ali saw, but he did not comment.

He was divine. And naughty. Even though we were on his turf, I was determined not let this sexy rooster rule the roost.

We enjoyed a sumptuous seafood platter.

Ali picked up a mussel. He asked me, "What does this remind you of?"

Naturally, I knew that he was referring to female anatomy. "I don't know," I said, "but don't you find them irresistibly gorgeous and delicious, especially with some white sauce and garlic?"

He flinched, then smiled with a look of admiration. Ali knew I was playing him at his own game. And not too badly either, I must say.

We continued our slight renegade conversation and discussed the effects of oysters on the libido.

"Do they affect women like they do men?" Ali quizzed me. "Let's find out. I suggest we finish the tray, then you tell me what happens to your loins, Mr Ali, and I will tell you whether anything happens to mine."

We settled into talking a bit about cars and the travel business. Ali told me about his time in Bristol. He met an Olympic horse rider, Annabelle. She was British and studied with him at the same university. They spent time together and become inseparable. It felt a bit like a threesome, Ali laughed, as the horse was more often with them than not. Naturally, Ali, as most well-to-do Arab men, rode too. They used to go off into the countryside surrounding Bristol, gallop- ing, and gallivant- ing around. On their rides, they dismounted their horses and mounted each other. They were glorious times.

They shared a great bond, Ali told me.

It later transpired that Ali's love, Annabelle, and her horse, Satchel, were up against Ali's family's stallion in the upcoming Olympics. Ultimately, the horse loyalty and taking equine sides ended up dividing them.

Had it not been for the Olympics, Ali felt, he might even now have been together with his English love. His British Rose.

After Ali recounted the story about Annabelle, he unexpect- edly asked,

"Did you ever love deeply?"

I must have looked bemused.

"Not in the friends and parental sense," he continued, "but in the "love sense", shall we say."

"Well, yes, of course," I said.

Why was Ali asking? He was married. I heard he had given his wife a massive pink diamond for her last birthday, and that he already had a few kids with more in the making.

"How is it to truly love?" he asked. "How is it to be free from expectations and be able to express your deepest emotions in the real sense of the word?"

"Well," I considered, "it hasn't happened to me often. But there was a time in my life when I could say I lost my heart to someone."

"What happened?" Ali asked.

"Do you want the short version or the long version?" I laughed.

"I want you to tell me enough to understand the journey of falling in love.

We have all afternoon. Please cancel your three o'clock appointment, Ms Vivika."

"Consider it cancelled, Mr Ali."

I began to tell Ali my story. "I had an encounter, many moons ago, with a handsome naval man.

I was still young and green at the time, though fairly feisty and independent, as I recall.

He was a captain, a commander, a pilot, an officer, and a gentleman.

My parents were friends with the British Consul General in Amsterdam.

148

When visiting British naval ships docked in the port, there would be a reception for dignitaries, and other essential invitees.

I attended these receptions frequently, with several of my single girlfriends.

These cocktail parties had been hosted on Her Majesty's ships since the time of Admiral Horatio Nelson, over two hundred years ago.

Commanders insisted these parties were necessary. Attending ministers, officials and councillors were seen to be impressed by British ships. It was said they would talk more freely than they might speak in more formal settings. There was also a morale-boosting aspect to the parties for the crew, as unattached local women could be invited.

And that is where we came in. Single Women."

"Nice," Ali contributed, as he smiled at the prospect of having a group of "vetted single women delivered to a party".

"You have me intrigued now, Ms Vivika. Tell me more."

"The ritual once onboard was as follows," I continued; "What can I get you ladies, to drink?" an officer would ask.

The first few times, it was a glass of wine or a gin and tonic. However, as we progressed, we learnt about other concoctions, including "Horse's Neck," a heady mix of brandy, ginger ale, and Angostura bitters, garnished with the curl of lemon peel from which it gets its name. Served to VIPs and ex-pats from a jug."

I checked in with Ali. *Was I boring him?*

"No, please Vivika, continue, I am all ears. Learning as I go along and charmed so far."

"I attended these cocktail parties on quite a few occasions. I knew the *Spiel*.

Living in Amsterdam at that time, I worked with a multi-national company.

I spent my days with foreign visitors. My evenings were taken up by my post-graduate marketing course.

They were full-on, and jam-packed days, getting up at dawn and going to bed past midnight.

At the end of an incredibly hectic four-week stint, I had another cocktail party in the diary.

It was the very last thing I felt like doing. I could have apologised. Possibly.

But there was a new girl in our company. Her name was Larissa. She had heard some of the stories of the cocktail receptions on the visiting ships and how much fun we used to have.

She looked so keen when she listened to the stories that I said she was welcome to join on the next occasion.

Larissa had not yet made any friends. It was her first time living away from home. The prospect of this party was what she had been living for, ever since she was invited. It was in her diary, and it was the talk of every coffee break."

"How did your night pan out?" Ali asked.

I proceeded to tell him about meeting CJ, how he clocked me and cracked me from the get-go.

Ali laughed when he heard about the G&T in my boot. I went on to tell him about the most extraordinary times we had together.

As I was talking to Ali, other adventures bubbled up from memory.

I told him about our stint in Gibraltar when Annie and I

stayed at The Rock Hotel. Captain James and his officers were on a royal mission to Cyprus.

"Annie and I met CJ *en route*, on their stop before entering the Mediterranean.

We spent a few days together in Gibraltar, or Gib as it was referred to.

Annie, CJ and Humphrey, one of the officers and I, went off in a tiny Ford Fiesta. We found a fantastic place for lunch across the border in Spain. Slightly boozed up, we tried to find our way back to Gibraltar, but got caught in the snow in the Sierra Nevada."

I took a sip of my water.

"What a story," Ali said. What happened next?" I paused.

"What happened to Captain James?" Ali asked again.

I continued.

"Even though we were no longer lovers, his spouse found out that he came to see me when I was in Switzerland for a job. James had been in France for training. His gruesome-sounding hard-core survival course took place just across the border in France. James had replied that it would be rude not to meet for fondue and catch up, not fondue and fondle. I told him I would love that.

Some years ago, I decided that, although I deeply loved James, I would no longer sleep with him. The fact that I had learnt that he was happily married stopped me from pursuing that aspect. Yes, we had a thing in the past. It stopped years and years ago. Sexually speaking, I mean. Intimacy wise, we were still as deeply bonded as ever."

"What happened after all of this?" Ali asked. "Do you still see each other?"

I took a deep breath and launched into my least favourite part as it related to "The Story of James", which was the part that marked "The End".

"Some weeks after I saw James in Switzerland, I received an email from him.

The title of the email was "This is not a good message".

I instantly smiled when I saw an email from James, assuming that the title referred to a joke or some outrageous situation he had experienced. He never disappointed, and the communications were hilariously entertaining. It was always a treat to hear from him.

I settled down with a cup of coffee and my laptop, ready to be entertained by James.

My smile was quickly wiped off my face as I read the mail, saying not to contact him. He went on to write that his wife thought we were having an affair. In his email, James elaborated further, noting that while we had the best of times and while I was the closest of friends, he could not compromise on his marriage. He could not lose the woman he loved and had loved from day one."

"Then what?" Ali asked.

"I was utterly distraught. I loved James deeply. Out of my true love and deep respect, I followed his wishes. I never contacted him again. I did not google him, track him or search for him. My loss was too profound.

The twenty-second kiss on the deck of HMS *Carlington*, all those years ago, had turned in to twenty incredible years of deep love and friendship. In many ways, James was the most significant person in my life. A treasure.

I chose to cherish our times and respect his position and

wish. I never contacted him again, though he, of course, stayed in my heart and was often on my mind.

Maybe that sounds unbelievable, but it is the God's honest truth."

"How long ago was that?" Ali asked.

"I think about two and a half or maybe three years ago or so. I can't quite remember. It was beyond sad. But what to do? I never intended to break anything. Had I known he was happily married,   I would never have let myself get close to him from the beginning."

I sighed and pondered the time that had passed since our last encounter.

Even though I knew it was not right, things happened. Life happened. Lust happened. Love happened.

The impact that James had on me would never be erased nor forgotten. My life would have been far less fun and vibrant without this amazing man.

I would never have known that there are men who can spark energies in you that you didn't know you had. Before James, I never knew that kind of man existed. He was the single most important man, in terms of love, in my entire life.

"I can see this was an emotional adventure and a lesson in love and in life," Ali said.

"But really, Vivika, it's a while back, and you were super close friends. Where is he now?"

"I just don't know; I have no idea."

"I think you should at least look him up. Surely a search on Google is worth a shot?" Ali concluded.

Dusk was upon us. It had been the most glorious afternoon, Very unexpected and enjoyable in a warm and valuable sort of way.

It was clear that Ali, too, had thoroughly enjoyed spending time together.

"Ali, my apologies. I know you asked a question about love and life, but I am quite sure you did not expect to be exposed to such a lengthy and intense story."

"Ms Vivika, you have no idea where you took me. Thank you for trusting me with your experience and your emotions. You touched me. I would like to thank you for sharing something so dear to your heart. I am humbled. At the same time, I feel happy to know you a bit better. Jump in the car with me, and I will drive you home," he said.

"But promise me one thing. Let me know where that Captain of yours is. Tell me what happens."

Ali dropped me off, thanked me for my time and wished me good night.

I went up to my apartment on the top floor. I looked out over the sea.

It was entirely still, like a giant lake. It looked at peace.

The silver moonlight reflected off the water. It was serenely beautiful.

Sparked by the afternoon's conversation, James was at the forefront of my mind.

Oh James, how you would have loved this pad. How I miss you still.

Rest in Peace

I took a shower and changed into my light cotton joggers and a T-shirt.

Having poured myself a glass of rosé, I decided to ask Doctor Google where Captain James was. I tapped in some keywords including *Carlington*, Navy, James Bowen-Jones, HMY *Britannia*, and then hit "search".

I was keen to know where James may be.

It would not hurt if I knew, as long as I did not contact him, I thought.

In shock, I realised I had landed on an obituary page.

There it was in front of my eyes. The announcement read, "RIP - Rest in Peace, Captain Bowen-Jones. Our sincerest condolences to the Bowen-Jones family; what a fabulous man he was".

The words were swirling in front of me. I could not focus.

I read and re-read the lines over and over. The words didn't equate in my brain.

My head spun. I felt dizzy, slumping down on the nearest couch.

In total disbelief, I just sat there.

Looking over the peaceful sea, the realisation started to set in. Emotionally and physically, I felt sick.

What happened? The fittest man on the planet. How could this be? Was it really him?

I reached out via LinkedIn to one of his trusted officers, and he confirmed the loss.

"What a guy," he replied. "What a leader. He will be forever missed. The fact that we lost such a great man to a heart murmur is heart wrenching and utterly unspeakably sad. May he RIP."

It was true.

James was dead.

I did not know where to turn.

To steady myself and to remember that Captain James Bowen- Jones really existed and had been very real in my life, I searched for the emails he had sent.

The memories of James and our times together instantly came flooding back.

In one email, James had written, "Hi Hun, Just got back from flying to Edinburgh this Sat morning. Been up in London for annual dinners."

I read his words and instantly felt James' presence as if nothing had changed. Whenever I received his emails or hand-written letters, through the British Forces postal services, my heart would instantly lift, and I would be ready to smile and be amused.

The stories and anecdotes were always funny, poignant, and exciting—a reflection of the man himself.

I found James captivating, even after all these years. Every time I saw him, spoke to him, or heard from him, I could be sure that the time would be epic and positively memorable.

I continued reading.

Even when James was entertaining me, his approach was systematic.

The email went on; Our activities over recent times.

1) Fleet Air Arm pissy-cacky-poo reunion dinner at our usual spot. Dinner average finished at mid-nightish. Then went to all manner of nightclubs, to roll into bed around 6-ish after a power breakfast at Smithfield's market. My mates all left me then to go home. You have got to know them all over the years, Woodston, Hover, Felix et al. Very naughty boys in their day!!! I, of course, had to stay another night for dinner number two.

2) Reunion dinner at Royal Thames Yacht Club (just down from Hyde Park and our famous hotel!).

I stopped reading and thought back to our time at "our famous hotel" just down from Hyde Park.

We met up in London. I was in the Middle East and had business in London, which coincided with CJ being in town for the Reunion Dinner. We agreed to meet at my hotel. I gave him my room number and advised security to allow him up. James arrived past midnight, all dressed up as usual, in Black Tie, looking handsome, very naval, and, naturally, arrived a bit boozed up.

He knocked on the door and hugged me and held me close like I had not seen him for ages, which was the case. He kept holding me and stroking my hair and kissing my head. "Blosh, here you are. What a total delight to see you."

James handled his drink very well and never lost control. He was just even funnier and fluid as well as a bit more "hands-on".

"Well, well, who has been shopping?" James said.

He proceeded to empty the Thomas Pink bag, which was on the chair by the desk and put it on his head as if he were a musketeer.

He proceeded to break into a march around the room.

With the bag still perched on his head, he stopped in front of me and sprang to attention, saluting me.

"I am your soldier, your officer and your special forces protector. Your wish is my command."

I remember laughing and saying, "You are indeed my very favourite officer and gentleman."

He slipped off his "Pink Top Hat" and settled down in the big plush, purple-coloured sofa in the corner of the room.

"Come here," he said, patting the space next to him.

I settled into the crook of his arm, where I always felt both happiness and comfort.

"Tell me," I said. "I want to hear all about you and your evening."

"It was a brilliant dinner," he told me. "Excellent food, superb wine and terrific company.

The after-dinner speech described us Royal Yacht Officers' Club as rather "like cut flowers in a vase. Beautiful specimens but doomed to die eventually"."

"Oh, my Lord," I exclaimed. "How crass. Can't believe the speech guy used that analogy, though it is a visual one, my petal."

Laughing, James squeezed me. "To be fair, we are a club that will never regenerate as there are no other Royal Yacht officers behind. No more Royal Yacht!"

I continued to read the email in front of me.

"Moore and Miller were on spectacular form and wished to be remembered to you. Loads to tell. Probably better over a landline, but few pics for you to look at. More later, CJXXXXXXXXXXXXXXX.

I could not stop my tears. My heart was in pain. The fact that James was gone forever gently started to sink in.

I continued to read another email from James, which read, "Hi, Hun, out on convoy with the boss so can't skype now. Thanks for your birthday wishes. You never forget. We have lots to talk about. But first things first - you OK? I have been whisked off to some Godforsaken part of the world where there aren't even any mob phone masts. Hence, sitting in the field with a laptop on my legs, tapping away and storing this email. I shall then, when I'm flying around the scrub, find a town where there is some broadband Wi-Fi and see if I can get a signal strong enough to send it to you. I'm drafting this at 1850 on Friday evening. God knows when you'll get it. Will talk when I get back from convoy. Love and squeezes to you, CJXXXXXXXXXX

I read and re-read his messages and allowed my thoughts and emotions to flow. I must have sat and cried and reminisced for quite some time.

Later that night, I sent a message to Ali.

"Dear Ali", I omitted "Mr". We had moved beyond that.

"As you suggested, I asked Doctor Google about Captain James. I was shocked and very saddened to learn that he passed away.

Thank you for your suggestion. It was because of you that I searched for him. Now I know.

Captain James is dead.

May his soul rest in eternal peace. It is surreal and bizarre, and I am stunned at the news."

Ali was quick to respond. "I am coming", he texted. "You need company at this time".

It sounded caring and kind. I was OK, and perhaps even relieved at the thought.

"What floor are you on?" "Top floor", I answered.

Within fifteen minutes, Ali arrived, dressed in a refreshed, bright white, immaculately pressed dish-dash.

He looked concerned and, at the same time, very handsome. I sat with my knees up under my chin, on the balcony bench.

"I am so sorry," Ali said.

Then he bent down and kissed me gently.

I prepared some mint tea, and we settled down on the balcony. The moonlight on the sea was serenely beautiful. I hoped James was at peace and still shining his awesome light from his place in heaven.

"I love talking to you," Ali said.

"Thank you for taking the time to come over and for being the reason for me finding out what I did. Had you not nudged me, I would have continued to think that James was alive.

I feel strangely and deeply re-connected with him now he is no longer with us. Now, imposed rules and requests not to contact him no longer apply.

Weirdly enough, that gives me a sense of peace. The painful thought of not being able to be in touch with James is now no longer relevant nor valid.

I can now talk to him whenever I like, in any circumstance and remember everything about him.

Thank you, Ali, for today."

Ali stayed for a while longer. We moved to the sofa inside. He sat next to me and pulled me into him. He stroked my hair.

I felt the warmth of his body and felt comfortable and comforted.

I know he was aroused. His dish-dash did not conceal the contours of his rock-hard manhood.

Ali, of course, realised I had noticed and joked, "Must have been those oysters we had for lunch."

There was no embarrassment, no urgency, and he didn't push for anything else.

Ali offered friendship. He was a gentleman.

True gentlemen are rare to find.

Ali stood up and said, "Are you alright, Vivika? I like your company. I think you are a proper and genuine person. You are a breath of fresh air."

"Thank you for coming, Ali. That was kind and hugely appreciated."

I walked him to the door, where he held me close and gently kissed me, a bit longer this time. I kissed him back.

Then Ali opened my front door, turned back to me and said, "Get some sleep, *habibti* Vivi. I will see you tomorrow at the hotel." His dark, deep frown seemed to be taking me in.

Then he left, down the corridor, towards the elevator.

Dating Disclosures

Having spent some years in Abu Dhabi, I was approached for a job in Europe, but looking after the MENA region, which was the Middle East, North Africa and included Europe. That suited me perfectly.

It was time to move on from "FabDab".

Ali and I were firm friends. Priscilla was a Posse Puss, and I felt there was the promise of continuity. I knew we would stay connected mostly since much time would still be spent in the UAE as part of my new job.

I was ready to get a bit more London into my life, but not give up on the Middle East. A fusion of both worlds struck me as utterly blissful.

It was great to have Annie to play with in London, and Helene, just a hop, skip and a jump away in Amsterdam.

I re-installed myself in my London pad and picked back up where I had left off. I had a few days in England, before kicking off my new job.

The first day in my new role would be in Dubai, at a company meeting. I was looking forward to the new challenge and, in the meantime, I was going to enjoy London life and getting re-connected. I met up with Josie and Rosalind at "Bros Brothers", a wine bar in St James', just off Pall Mall. They were a good laugh. I had met them while working for the airline, ages ago when I first lived in London.

Rosalind, or Rosie as we called her, was a vixen. A true man-eater.

Her stories were always shocking, yet very entertaining. Rosie had recently split from her long-term boyfriend, Richard Deville-Daring, or "Darling Dicky", as she called him.

Rosie and Dicky had only been an item, for just over two weeks.

For Rosie, that was definitely long-term. Come to think of it, anything over two days was considered long-term for Rosie. Rosie launched into her latest news flash on the "love front". "Girls. I split up with Darling Dicky. I managed to enjoy him for almost two and a half weeks. There is no reason to cry over spilt milk, though I must admit, I did so like Dicky's.

I quite miss coming home to that."

"EEK," Josie gasped. "Too much info, Rosie."

"OK," she said.

"Let me tell you where this is heading. I decided I must simply get over Dicky by seeing someone else. You know, go on the rebound and all that. I thought I should explore some of the dating Apps. I tried my luck on Grindr."

"Grindr?" We gasped, in unison.

"I know, I got it wrong the first time," Rosie said. "I did not know that it was a hardcore gay thing. So, I educated myself and moved over to the heterosexual, though still rampant one."

She paused for breath and continued, "It's called Tinder." Rosie took a swig of her wine and continued,

"Girls, what an invention. It is like being in a candy store and being able to pick whoever you fancy. I had a blast over the past month.

I must remember to keep it a secret from Mummy. She may well follow suit and start dating guys half my age, from the comfort of her *chaise-longue*, no doubt.

As you know, Mummy and Daddy have always had a very open relationship. I am convinced that Daddy is at it like a rabbit.

I spotted the Tinder app on his phone. Can you imagine?

How cool is that? Both father and daughter, on the same dating app."

Josie and I were mortified.

"Rosie, you can't be serious," Josie said.

As for me, I just couldn't talk, I had to laugh so much. Once I recovered, I said, "But Rosie, he is your Dad."

"Yes, I realise that" she said, "but what to do? Men are hunters. It is in their DNA. If they say they are not doing it, you are simply a fool to believe them. They live to conquer. They hunt to kill. And I, for one, will not attempt to stop the male species from what they do best. I shall simply flutter around and enjoy every one of them, as they land me as their prey."

"Stop it," Josie pleaded. "I will pee my pants laughing."

Rosie then asked me, "So, pray, do tell, Vivikins, have you ever "Tindered"?"

"I have," I said. "I am a total Tinder Pro." "Tell us," both Rosie and Josie exclaimed.

"First, we need another round of drinks," I said, "as you may

164

have to limber up a bit. This is a story you have not yet been entrusted with."

"Come on, Vivi," Rosie said, "It is about time that I am not considered the only outrageous loose girl in our threesome. I have been carrying that burden alone for too long."

I settled into telling Rosie and Josie about my online dating experience.

"There was this Egyptian guy, Mohammad, or Maz, as I called him.

It was a relatively recent affair, when I was in Abu Dhabi.

One day, after work, I was relaxing on my balcony, having hung up with my girlfriend, Priscilla. She was the one who told me about Tinder.

Priss, as I called her, had broken up with her Arab Man and was exploring the world of online dating. I had no idea about any of it but thought I would give it a go. Priss told me it was great fun and more entertaining than reading a book or watching TV.

It didn't take long to get the hang of it. Tinder is all about visual selection.

I saw some scaries, some numpties, some notties and some hotties.

Maz was firmly in the latter category. He looked good and was an investment banker, living in Dubai.

He was quite a bit younger than me. But what did I care, I was a cougar on the prowl, exploring my online hunting ground, from the comfort of my Fab Pad, in Fab Dab, as I used to call Abu Dhabi.

When I saw Maz's picture, I swiped right, or was it left? Anyhow, we matched.

Our online profile pictures danced around each other, celebrating the alignment. It was an unexpected little thrill. Exciting somehow. A bit like winning an e-bay auction, having outsmarted the competition.

I soon realised that Tinder is a numbers game. Especially for guys. They try and match with the maximum number of possible people to increase their chances of dates and opportunities to indulge in whatever they are seeking. Sex mostly, as it turns out.

Maz and I started chatting, and we texted all night. Naturally, there was an ever-increasing degree of flirting and innuendo.

We continued to connect over the next week or so.

I made up raunchy scenarios and pretended that Maz was my counter character.

He loved it and could not get enough of the stimulating stories.

Then, the week came when he was going to meet me in Abu Dhabi.

Maz said, "If I come to see you, what will happen?"

I indulged in my best playwright mode and cobbled together a sexy string of events.

"So," he said, "when you hear me go ding-dong on your doorbell, all of that will happen? You will let me take you on the sofa, overlooking the sea from your top floor apartment? Then, we have shrimps and mojitos on the balcony, followed by a BJ for dessert?"

"Well, we shall see," I flirted.

"I'll be coming," he said.

"And that, my girls, he did," I said, giving them a suggestive wink and a broad grin.

"OMG," Josie formed the letters without any sound. Rosie stared at me, wide-eyed. "Go on, don't stop."

"The day came that Maz was due to visit for the first time. Oh Lord, I didn't know what to do with myself. I was playing with fire. We had texted tantalising scenarios for days and nights on end, but the fact remained that I had never met him. What if he were some out of control madman, I was planning on allowing into my house? Nonetheless, I gave him my address and sent him my location. At around eight o'clock in the evening, just as he said, the bell rang. I opened the door and was very pleasantly surprised by this virtual stranger with whom I exchanged virtual intimacies."

"Am I late?" Maz asked, as he made his way into my hallway and planted his rucksack in the corner under the coat rack. He looked smart in his pin-stripe suit and pale blue tie.

"I came straight from work," he said. "Hope you don't mind."

During our chats, Maz told me that he was an investment banker.

Naturally, I said, "Oh, no."

He was surprised, and texted back, saying, "Usually being an investment banker is a selling point on Tinder".

"Not for me," I messaged back. "I am not usually drawn to investment wankers, but let's see how you measure up, despite your handicap."

"Maz was a highly intelligent guy and rolled with the punches. The banter between us was an aphrodisiac, but I did not know whether the sex-appeal would be there when we met in person."

"Go on," Rosie said, "I want to hear all the gory details in all their splendour."

"Well, after our initial few minutes of introduction, Maz took off his jacket and tie and hung them in the hallway. He asked if he could use the bathroom. When he came out, he did not say anything, but pulled me into him and kissed me hard. He then smiled at me, took my hand and walked me from the hallway to the living room.

"This is the sofa you were talking about, isn't it?"

Then, right there, in my living room, he undressed me, and indulged me fully."

Rosalind and Josie gasped.

"He just took me, girls. Maz handled me like an expert and that, I guess, he was.

I must say that I reconsidered my stance on investment bankers, especially after I experienced that he could "return on his investment", after an hour or two," I laughed.

Both Rosalind and Josie were fully absorbed in the story and lost in the moment.

I continued.

"I made the shrimps which we enjoyed on the balcony. Then I gave the boy a BJ for dessert.

We talked for hours. Maz was an eloquent and knowledgeable conversationalist.

As I said, he had a bright mind and a sharp sense of humour. Maz was a risk-taker and a fast and smooth mover.

That was the beginning of an intense four-month rollercoaster relationship.

One day, we were in Dubai. I met up with Maz at his office, in one of the banking towers. We set off in his car to go for lunch. The security officer saw us leaving the building and observed us going down the ramp of the bank's parking garage.

"Why is he looking at us so intently?" I asked Maz.

"Well, you are blonde, and that means you are my latest bit of crumpet," he laughed.

"Those security guys wish they could have anyone as gorgeous as you. Unfortunately for them, you are out of their league. And, happily for me, you are in mine."

"You truly are an investment wanker," I said, "you conceited little shit." I chastised him.

"Language, Viv," he said. "Be polite now. There is no need to throw insults at me, especially as I am taking you to an excellent place for lunch."

After lunch, Maz went to the bathroom. I decided to pick up the bill.

When he came back, he wanted to settle the check, but I had already paid. It seemed a nice thing to do. Rather than saying "thank you", he went mad, Arab style.

I learnt right there and then that for a Middle Eastern man, you do not pick up the check, or even split the bill. It is an insult if a woman does that to a man. I may as well have called him inadequate. He felt utterly emasculated.

Here's a tip, girls. Don't do it. Do not pay for lunch."

Rosie and Josie seemed to be lapping it up, so I thought I would take things a little further.

"Maz and I lasted for some time. He liked it when I dressed up in different outfits and danced for him."

"You danced for him?" Rosie and Josie said at the same time.

I did not answer but continued.

"One day, there was a World Cup football match on T.V.

I was dancing for him in my red lacquer Agent Provocateur outfit. He was not sure where to spend most of his time looking, at the semi-final world-cup football match, or at me. He was a massive football fan. But in the end, he opted for me, over the football.

After we "finished", I went to wash up in the bathroom and found a packet with blue pills, next to the sink. I was flummoxed. In total shock. *What was going on?* I couldn't think straight.

That was the first encounter with Viagra.

Utterly confused and with anger rising, I marched in with the tablet box in my hand. When Maz was within reach, I threw the pills at him and said, "Did you need this to have sex with me?"

"No, of course not," he answered.

"Then why is it here?" I spat back.

He was blatant and said, "You are not my last call for the night".

"No, he did *not* say that Viv," Josie exclaimed.

"He jolly well did," I replied. "I went totally ape, as you can imagine."

Rosalind and Josie were hanging on my every word. "Then what?" Rosie urged me to continue.

"I laid into him saying, "Who the hell do you think you are? You should have that sad appendage of yours, which supposedly reflects your manhood, cut off and put in pickle juice. You are no man to me. You are a disgusting weasel from hell."

I gave him a total earful and scolded myself for being such an unbelievably sad and feeble fool."

"What did he do and what did he say and what could he possibly have replied?" Josie asked.

"Maz raised his voice at me and said "Stop, *ya Hilloueh*",

which means stop sweetie, or pretty one. He came towards me and tried to hold me.

I pushed him away and moved to the other side of the sofa to create a physical barrier between us.

He went on to say, "*Majnooneh*", "Crazy One" and tried to pacify me by saying,

"Calm down, my sexy Dutch girl".

I screamed at him and hurtled every offensive word in my very extensive foul vocabulary at him. "I know I may not be in an official relationship with you, but this takes the biscuit! You wanker!" I screamed at him. "You probably take Viagra to have sex with multiple women. You are a pathetic, spineless piece of *khara.*"

I paused for breath, and interjected, "That, girls, means "poo", or more appropriately in this case, "shit" in Arabic."

I could see that they were impressed. I continued. "I was so furious I cried."

"Don't cry," he said. "Give me that gorgeous smile of yours. I don't want my girl to be upset."

"I am not your girl," I spluttered.

"Yes, you are," he said. "You are my Anglo-Dutch girl, and you are wild and crazy and a bit explosive, but I like that, my blue-eyed bomb."

In a swift leap, he jumped over the sofa, grabbed me around the waist and started kissing my cheek. I fended him off.

"Listen," he said, "Let's forget all this shitty nonsense and let me take you into the desert tomorrow. We are going with the 4x4 club, and I want you to come.

I will show these ranger friends of mine, what a real woman looks like."

"I hate you," I said.

"I know," he replied. "I am a big *khara*. I don't expect you to believe me when I say you mean a great deal to me, but you do. Come with me tomorrow. I will go and get everything we need and pick you up at seven o'clock in the morning, as it will be hot and we need an early start. Let me make it up to you for being a shithead and let me give you a great time tomorrow. You will love it. I know you will. Now, smile at me."

His cheeky grin and deep dark eyes were both mocking and encouraging.

I couldn't help but give him the smallest of smiles through my tears.

"I take that as a yes," Maz said, "We leave tomorrow morning at seven on the dot."

At precisely seven o'clock, Maz called me.

"Vivi, grab your stuff and meet me down in the garage underneath your building. I parked next to the elevator so you will see me when you come out.

I am filling up the water and checking the oil. Can you bring me an extra bottle of tap water, in case we need it in the desert, for whatever reason? Best to be prepared."

I realised how Maz was fully engaged with the trip.

Making sure all the equipment was checked and fit for action, Maz was a man on a mission.

His modified Jeep was stocked with water, a full jerry can of petrol, spades, ropes, and Lord knows what else. The hidden mini-fridge, which was built into the vehicle in such a way that most police officers would not notice it, was fully stocked.

A Muslim married man, caught with alcohol in a car with a blonde girl, was not a scenario that would go down well with the authorities. Without the alcohol being found, he would have a fair chance of being able to continue on his way unencumbered.

We drove to a designated petrol station to meet the other people, all with their fully equipped 4x4s, who would join the expedition. I spoke to the other rangers when we were gathering.

One of them, Nader, was from Jordan, now living in the UAE. I told Nader a bit about our Jordan adventure when we went with Annie, Martin, and Hélène.

We discussed the fantastic wonder of Petra and the vast stillness and beauty of Wadi Rum, or "Valley of the Moon", as it translates from Arabic. I camped overnight there and was bowled over by the beauty of the desert. We chatted easily. I thought nothing else of it.

Nader said that he would be delighted to give me some more tips for adventures in Jordan and that if I ever went back again, I should let him know. With that, he scribbled his number on a piece of paper and handed it to me. He then asked for mine and loaded it directly into his mobile phone.

We spent an incredible day in the desert, driving the vehicles up very steep dunes and then almost floating down on the other side. It was exhilarating. We laughed, challenging each other. After we climbed a massive dune from the rear, ready to drive over the precipice, and slide down the other side, the car got stuck. Maz manoeuvred the Jeep expertly and managed to get it going again.

Sliding down the other side was an utter thrill.

At the bottom of the descent, we got stuck again, but this time, more efforts were required.

The packed spades made an appearance and Nader came to the rescue in his 4x4.

Maz was fixing the tow rope to the relevant parts of Nader's car to try and move the Jeep.

As they were digging to try and get the wheel out, I jumped out of the Jeep to see if I could assist in any way. The sand was so excruciatingly hot underfoot, that I leapt straight back into the car, shouting profanities as I launched myself back in through the open passenger door.

"Bloody hell, that is insane."

I noticed Maz, looking at me. He was laughing. "You OK, Viv? Heat is just a perception. I thought that you could manage more than this, my crazy Dutch girl," Maz gave Nader a manly wink as he said it.

"Somehow, it felt like he was sending Nader a message, though I could not quite put my finger on what, or why," I told Rosie and Josie.

After a fabulous day, which was relaxed and a whole lot of fun, we made our way back towards civilisation. It was 48 degrees Celsius as we moved out of the desert just before the sun went down—such crazy heat. The air is so hot, you burn yourself breathing.

We made a stop at the mosque in a tiny village, on the edge of the desert.

The guys parked their Jeeps and Landrovers and made their way into the local mosque for sunset, Maghreb prayers. We then continued our way.

Maz asked me what the Jordanian Ranger, Nader, had said to me.

I told him we chatted about our trip to Jordan and that he offered to help next time we were planning to go.

Maz went on to ask me whether Nader asked me for my number.

I told him he gave me his mobile number on a piece of paper and asked me for mine and logged it in his phone.

When he heard this, Maz went mad. He called Nader and ordered him to park the car at the roadside under the next bridge. Nader obliged and stopped his vehicle.

Maz overtook him and parked in front of Nader and got out of the Jeep.

I adjusted the rear mirror so I could see what was going on behind me.

Nader had already opened the window. Maz put his head right through it and started shouting at Nader, mere centimetres from his face.

Maz's body language was very aggressive. He was clearly filled with explosive testosterone.

After some minutes, I saw Nader give his mobile phone to Maz, who proceeded to press several buttons. Rather than giving the mobile back to Nader, Maz demonstratively threw the phone back into Nader's car.

After a few more minutes and animated conversations, Nader opened the car door and came out. I waited with bated breath to see what would happen.

Were they about to have a fight?

Nader said a few more words to Maz and then offered his hand, which Maz took and shook. Then they gave each other a "man hug" and slapped each other on the shoulder. Maz came back to the Jeep, and both cars started moving again.

"What was that all about?" I asked.

"How dare he ask for your number!" Maz roared. "Mother fucker! We don't hunt each other's women. How dare he? He knows you are mine and that you belong to me. He was out of order, and I told him so in no uncertain terms. I deleted your number from his phone and told him never to contact you. And if he does, I expect you to block him and to tell me."

It turned out Nader had apologised to Maz, acknowledging that he had overstepped the boundaries of respect. He had said he thought I was "just a friend", and that they always "tried their luck with any new girl in the desert".

In the end, the territorial boundaries were set. Nader had been warned off Maz's Turf.

Good God, I thought, remembering the situation, *that was a bit intense.*

At the same time, I was secretly satisfied, that Maz made it clear that I was not to be hunted, as I was already somebody else's trophy. Ridiculous, of course, I realise.

However, after the episode the day before with the Viagra violation, I was somehow pleased to see Maz fight for me. Even if it was a display of pride-infused cock dancing antics. I saw the rawness of male lashing out to a fellow species, like two lions fighting over one lioness.

This time, Maz staved off the competition. But he would be on the lookout for the next attack, as long as he remained interested in the prey.

"Wow and OMG!" Rosalind exclaimed. The girls looked at me, wide-eyed.

"All that was the result of Tinder, and swiping left, or was it right? That is so awesome," Rosalind sighed.

"Well," I said, "If you don't want to end up with a life made up of bland chapters which will bore you to tears in your old age, you better take a chance and pursue life. It is not always a happy story. Maz messed me up, although we had some excellent times.

I cried more than is usual in any relationship. But in the end, I have a story. An experience. We enjoyed some sweetness and spice, and I learnt some lessons along the way."

Volcanic Vilifications

I arrived in Dubai, on the overnight flight from London, which lasted approximately seven hours.

I was to start my new job at the annual meeting. I thought that sounded perfect.

I imagined I would meet everyone and listen to the updates of the team members and the leaders of the group. Apparently, the owner and his consultant would be there too.

I made it through customs and was met on the other side by a man with a sign saying, "Ms. Vivika – Damsonite Properties".

I knew that Damsonite was the owning company and was happy that the meeting arrangements had worked out.

"Please, Ms Vivika," the driver offered, "allow me."

Having taken my luggage, he handed me a cold face towel and a choice of iced or room temperature bottled water.

"Thank you," I said, accepting the cold water. "What is your name?" I asked.

"Majdi," he answered and opened the back door for me to get in.

"Thank you, Majdi," I said and settled into a smart-looking

car, noticing the number plate "DP 10", clearly one of the Damson Properties' fleet.

We sped off to a location which was around half an hour from Dubai airport. I just about recognised The Creek and the Jumeirah area. The place had changed so much since Annie's and my trip.

The one thing that did immediately hit me was the heat and the level of humidity. Even underground car parks were fully air-conditioned in Dubai, I remembered.

We arrived at the building where the meeting would take place. I was greeted by the CEO and some of my new colleagues. We settled down around the u-shaped meeting table—all seventeen of us.

The chatter died down and subsided as he walked in. He was the boss. Everyone knew it except me.

He was a commanding man, tall and handsome in a rugged, yet refined sort of way.

He wore a turban in vibrant turquoise and tangerine, carefully knotted around his head, Omani style.

Clad in traditional Arabic dress, his kandura was pristine, bright white and crisply pressed. Not a crease in sight, apart from down the sleeves, where they were both pronounced and intended.

It fascinated me how men in white stepped out of their chauffeur-driven expensive cars and looked as if they never sat down, their impressive garments perfectly intact.

The "man with a presence", nodded to the assembled company, who immediately responded with murmurs of respect and awe.

He settled into his chair.

Someone dedicated to the job of making sure his seat was positioned exactly as needed, pulled his "throne" out and ensured he took his position in what clearly was "The Driving Seat".

"Welcome." He spoke loudly and clearly, with great authority. There was no warmth in his voice. I think hostility, would be a more appropriate description.

"We are here to discuss your performance. Or should I say, lack of it?" Boss-Man started.

"As the owner, along with my partner, we are concerned that you are not equipped to deliver on your projected returns. You are far less professional and competent than you make yourselves out to be. We signed a management agreement with you some three years ago and, by Jove, you really have let yourselves down, as well as my business partner and me, in the process."

I was taken aback, both by Boss-Man's British accent and his outspoken manner.

He was clearly well-educated, eloquent, and very unhappy with the business, as well as with the company I had just joined. "It seems to me that you have severely oversold yourselves and dramatically and catastrophically under-delivered. The time has come to address the situation in no uncertain terms," Boss-Man thundered.

"You are here to tell me exactly what will happen and how you will be delivering on your promises, within what time-frame and against which budget. Speaking of budget, you have already squandered most of it. I would say that the allocated finances have gone against alcohol consumption, to oil the cogs of your management. In this context, management is a term I use loosely, as no results have been forthcoming. The only dent you have made is in the number of bottles that disappeared from my wine cellar. Perhaps it is the very consumption of the heavenly fluid that has brought out the worst in you.

I have brought you here, at my expense once again, to awaken you from your hibernation and your inebriation. You have been sleeping, it appears. We are your owners. While you are snoozing, snoring, and drooling, you are giving us sleepless nights.

You, and I mean every single one of you, are the very matter nightmares are made of."

He looked up at the skies and raised his arms, a gesture of despair, which clearly seemed to befit his feelings.

He continued.

"I am all ears to hear what fantasies and incredulous justifications, you will undoubtedly be serving up today.

Scarlet Pimpernel, why don't you kick off and tell us exactly why you have crashed and burned. Even though you wear a flame of Irish Auburn on your pale and pretty head, you clearly do not house much grey matter on the inside. Shame really Redhead. It would have been nice to have exquisite looks and smart thoughts. Clearly, the two will never meet. Or at least not in you."

Wow, what a killer bastard. Whatever next?

After an uneasy shuffling, the Vice President of Sales, Shannon, who was my boss, broke the silence.

"Your Excellency," she started "it has been a tough start for us all.

There were many delays in finalising the opening of the three latest resorts. The team has been working day and night. However, with the dust storms of recent weeks and the organisational changes and challenges, we have fallen behind. We assure you, we will catch up."

"Dust storms!" he bellowed.

"Are you seriously blaming your lack of ability to perform what you are paid to do on "dust storms"?"

"Let me remind me that I led my troops during Operation Desert Storm, back in the early '90s. It was a war. No one ever used "dust storms" as an excuse not to get the job done. My people committed to what was needed. We pulled together, along with our international allies, and conquered.

I was educated and trained to the highest standards and led my various squadrons through most demanding circumstances over a great many years.

In my wildest dreams, I could not have imagined that, some-day, I would be relegated to dealing with the sorry bunch of spineless professionals I see before me today."

Utter silence.

Boss-Man lit up a cigarette and stared at every one of us.

When he got to me, he clearly did not know who I was. "Who are you? Do tell," he said.

Shannon jumped in.

"We have recently appointed a new Head of Regional Sales, to develop business and lead the sales team," she said.

"Have you, indeed?" he said in a steely voice.

I couldn't quite decide whether his expression was sardonic or ironic.

He turned his eyes to me and said, "Oh pray, do tell. Who are you? Did you land from the heavens? Are you the latest Supreme Saviour from Definite Disaster?"

He paused. For effect, no doubt.

Then he turned to "Redhead" as he called Shannon.

"How is she different from all those who went before? And why is it that, after my repeated instructions on the topic of hiring, you have still failed to let me vet your new recruits?"

Another pause.

He looked at me and said, "How long have you been with this group of utterly incompetent self-congratulating, impotent and ineffective leaders, whom I have heavily invested in, without any type of encouraging results or outcomes?"

He slammed his hand on the table. We all jolted and sat bolt upright.

"From under which rusty stone did they pull you, to embark on turning around their sad and ineffective strategies?"

Shannon looked desperate.

"Your Excellency, Vivika is very experienced."

And then, locking her pleading gaze on to me, she said, "Please, introduce yourself."

I stood up and spoke.

"Good morning. Thank you for inviting me to your annual meeting. This is "day one" for me. I look forward to contributing to a positive uplift in the business."

There was total silence in the full room, followed by the voice of thunder.

"Are you from Australia?" he barked.

"Spare me the Australians. Or are you South African? One is no better than the other. Where do you come from?"

"I am European - a mix. Dutch and British," I said.

"Never mind," he shouted.

"Clearly, you will need about a year to settle in to "get to know" the company. Then you will blame external issues and question internal challenges. After twelve months, you will be equally deficient, pathetic, and as useless as these spineless blobs. And then you, too, will slide down the spiral into nothingness, to join these sad excuses of human beings, and continue to plummet into oblivion and despair. Except, I will not allow for that to happen."

He looked at the sky.

"*Ya, Allah!*" A term of despair, to emphasise he had reached the end of his patience, meaning "my dear God".

He grabbed a cigarette.

The man on his right, quick as a flash, pulled out a lighter and lit him up. He sucked on the cigarette and inhaled deeply. The smoke stayed inside him. Then, he took his time to exhale.

This man was like a volcano, though to say he was explosive would be an understatement.

He dragged on his cigarette a few more times and then stubbed it out. Settling back into his tirade, Boss-Man continued.

He now directed his words to the CEO of the group.

"Your incompetence will see your company being de-flagged from my resorts. Your name will be dis-associated from my mine and all I control in this part of the world."

Then, turning to the frail, pale thin and dark-eyed middle-aged woman next to Shannon, he said,

"Squirrel, what fabulous figures do you have to share? I never equated finance with frigidity. However, looking at you, I cannot think of them in isolation."

The room fell silent once again.

"Give it to us, Miss Accountability. What is your bottom

line?"

He stopped to drink water and gulped down the replenished glass in one go.

"You should have been hired by a non-profit organisation. You don't appear to understand the concept of making money to cover expenses and go beyond. You are alien to the thought of growth and expansion. I am not sure whether to pity or despise you."

Just at that time, the call to prayer muffled his words. Respectfully, he silenced his rant and spoke the relevant words under his breath.

"*Allahu Akbar.*" God is most great.

He then pushed his chair back, throwing the "chair pusher and puller" off-balance, as he leapt off to perform *Wudu*, the ritual washing in preparation for prayers and worship.

"Twenty minutes break," he said. With that, he was gone.

After prayers, coffee and the regular cigarette break, the meeting proceeded, at a steady, less threatening pace.

There were fewer insults, more questions, and more even-keeled comments.

When nine and a half hours later, the meeting ended, Boss-Man spoke.

"You have failed to impress me.

You have achieved only one thing, which has been to prevent me from going to my next business meeting. You best put your heads together, or those very same heads will roll."

He got up to leave the meeting room.

As he passed by me, he said, "When are you leaving Dubai?"

I said I would be on the plane that night. He looked at me

and said;

"Change your flight. Do you seriously think that I would accept the Head of Sales to leave without viewing the properties and discussing strategies with the owner?"

And then, across to his senior PA and office manager, he said, "Do what is needed and block two hours in my agenda each day over the next three days. I need to tell this young lady, in no uncertain terms, what is at stake here."

Off he stepped, all in white, brandishing a cigarette, followed by his scrambling entourage

Limbo Leisure

It had been one hell of a first day on the new job.

I was not able to spend any time getting to know my colleagues, nor did I receive a briefing on anything. I had gone in stone cold and had come out fully fried.

After the meeting, Majdi picked me up and drove me to the resort where I'd be staying.

I had not received any details on the location and simply got in the car and fell asleep.

On arrival, I was dropped directly at what looked like a large luxury chalet.

At first glance, it appeared fantastic, but I was too exhausted to check it out.

I needed to sleep. I forced myself to clean my teeth, stripped off and fell into bed.

I woke up to the sound of a soothing gong.

I pulled the delicate cotton waffle dressing gown from the closet, put it on, and went outside.

On the terrace, leading out from my suite, was a moderately

sized but perfectly formed private plunge pool. Breakfast was laid out in the shade under the superior-looking parasol.

There were two choices of coffee, including a Turkish brew, with a hint of cardamom.

Caramelised dates, honey and exquisite fruits were laid out on a slab of slate, drizzled with pomegranate molasses. The freshly picked figs still had the morning dew on their green and blush pink skin. Two neatly poached eggs served with some well-prepared dark green spinach, perched perfectly on top of a freshly made wholegrain muffin, placed neatly on a pretty hand-painted plate.

Alongside, there was a clay vessel, in the shape of an Aladdin's lamp. It was glazed on the inside in deep turquoise and was filled to the brim with "Sauce Béarnaise".

On a long slim plate, giant capers, the size of marbles, were scattered over slices of wild salmon. A breakfast "Fit for a Queen". Taking it all in, I sat in the sunshine, sipping my coffee and indulging in the delicacies.

I thanked my lucky stars that I was back where I belonged. I slipped out of my bathrobe and into the perfect pool. Sun-rays warmed my face. With my boobs bobbing, legs kicking and a contented smile on my face, I was in heaven. How lovely could the morning of day two in a new job be?

One hundred and eighty degrees better than yesterday, I had to admit.

After a satisfying breakfast, I went in for a shower.

The red light on the phone was flashing. I called the operator. "A message for you to please meet with His Excellency, General Salim at 9.30. in reception, Ms Vivika." I thanked her and hung up.

Finally, I knew his title. Somehow it had not come up before. Everyone had simply called him "Your Excellency". Nobody introduced me to him. I did not know of his existence until he showed up. He was certainly not a "Silent Partner", that was for sure. Better get my skates on. What to wear?

I was in the lobby on the dot of 9.30.

General Salim was on the phone. He looked perturbed.

He acknowledged me with a curt nod, then he left through the door from where I had entered.

I sat down and took in my surroundings.

The lobby was scented with that intoxicating Omani Oud. I inhaled deeply.

I admired the school of dolphins made of driftwood.

They were positioned on poles of varying heights and appeared to be darting through the lobby. It was as if they were unaware, that when the ocean stopped, their habitat too ended.

Alongside the suspended school of frolicking mammals was a piano, which appeared to be made entirely out of shells. I felt like I was in a fantasy world. It was serene and utterly enchanting.

I leafed through the beautiful coffee-table books with extraordinary images of Oman. I could not wait to explore this great-looking country.

While I was waiting, I asked Doctor Google about Oud. I had never thought of looking it up before. I was fascinated to read that in the Middle East, "Oud" is known as black gold or *bakhoor*. The pungent and prized fragrance ingredient comes from one of the rarest and most expensive woods in the world. Arabia's nomadic Levantine tribes first used it thousands of years ago. They would set up camps, and burn Agar-wood to fragrance the air, and additionally to repel insects. As the scent is so heavy, it is sometimes blended with jasmine and sandalwood to soften and sweeten it.

In summer, the scent of Oud pervades Hyde Park, signifying the presence of the Arabs as they escape the summer heat in Arabia, and spend their time in London.

I remember the time Annie and I first smelt the evocative scent at the Emirates check-in desk at London Gatwick Airport, before we boarded our flight to Dubai.

I thought it was amazing then, and Oud still stirs me to my core today.

Having sat in the lobby waiting for General Salim to return, it dawned on me that he may not be coming back and that all that remained of him was his lingering scent.

Where was he?

The hotel manager, Pelle, confirmed my thoughts.

He was tall and Scandinavian-looking. His pale blue-green eyes could be described as "Eau de Nil". The colour reminded me of my much loved Fortnum and Mason classic tea tin and of my ceramic pot of "*Sal de Ibiza*", in the very same shade.

Clad from head to toe in crisp white, with a hint of pale blue linen, Pelle reflected the casual, yet high-quality character of the hotel.

"I am so sorry, dear Ms Vivika," Pelle said, as he made his way across the lobby.

"His Excellency, General Salim, had to leave so suddenly due to the passing of one of his family members. The lady in question was a prominent figure in society, as indeed all his family are. The various heads of state are flying in from the GCC countries and Europe. He asked me to pass on his apologies and to arrange for a proper show round and excursions and then to arrange for your flight back to London tonight."

"I am very sorry to hear that. Please would you be kind enough to convey my condolences to General Salim on my behalf?"

"Of course, Ms. Vivika. Thank you. In the meantime, can you please afford me half an hour to arrange your day? I will also have your flight changed. If agreeable to you, you will be picked up from your chalet, to experience our wonderful resort."

Sorry for your loss, General. At the same time, thank you for the opportunity not to be insulted and verbally abused. I think I would much prefer to go home than spend part of the next three days here, with you; no offence, Your Excellency.

I always thought in scenarios and could see them play out in my mind's eye. I did not have a good feeling about spending time with General Salim and be at the receiving end of his sharp tongue and overbearing way.

During the day, I inspected the resort.

Some of the most expensive bungalows were on the beach, overlooking the sea.

Then there were super-duper superior chalets, tucked away in oasis-style enclaves surrounded by date palms. I wasn't quite sure which I preferred. Both styles were glorious.

I was staying in the enclave. Private and secluded. Lush and lovely.

We picked herbs in the organic garden, grilled shrimp on the beach, went out on a boat, checked out the restaurants and enjoyed our time.

Saleh, the Experience Officer, accompanied me. He was a local and told me all sorts of interesting anecdotes and stories like only an "insider" can.

It was great to enjoy the day so much and still be able to call it "work".

Next up was the Spa.

After a tropical shower and light foot massage ritual, I lay down on the sumptuous massage bed, in the buff, face down, peeking through a hole left to breathe. A fresh fluffy white towel covered my bum.

I looked down on a lovely copper bowl, in which orchids were arranged. They were placed in a shallow amount of water, along with floating candles which released the subtle scent of jasmine. I glanced over my shoulder to see Omar, the masseur, cracking open a fresh coconut.

He dislodged and extracted the fresh white flesh of the *Joz Hind*, which translates from Arabic as "nut of India". He then proceeded to grate the flesh all over my body, the treatment that can only be described as an exquisite hybrid between scrub and massage.

After my "coconut experience", Omar finished off the session by applying Frankincense oil, which boosts cell immunity.

I was intrigued by the history of frankincense. It was apparently considered the most precious commodity of ancient Arabia and was traded in the Arabian Peninsula for over six thousand years. Its appeal was so strong, that the Frankincense Trail in Oman's Dhofar Governorate was, so they say, visited by the notable explorers, Marco Polo and Lawrence of Arabia. After the massage, I was given a cup of exotic lemongrass and fresh ginger tea, with a dollop of pure organic honey from the local beehives.

The sugar boosted my energy level after my state of total relaxation.

I slowly got dressed and snacked on some dates and plump apricots, the size of golf balls, freshly picked from the resort's orchard.

I had an hour to pack my bag and go off to the airport. It was going to be quite a drive, but I didn't mind. After my royal treatment in the Spa, I was sure to have a good sleep on the flight.

My initial trip with the new company was interesting and exciting but also weird and disturbing.

The flight was uneventful. It departed and arrived as scheduled and took one hour longer than the flight in.

This is caused by something to do with "flying in the same way that the world spins", which means it takes longer than flying in the other direction.

I made my way back home, unpacked and fell into bed for a few hours, before starting my day in the UK.

Boss-Man

The following day, I went into the office in Central London, to meet the Team.

We spent some time on introductions and then revisited the business plans, goals, and strategies, and I took time and settled into my office.

My work-space was bright and uncluttered. I was happy to see jasmine and lavender growing from the window boxes outside my office. The sunlight flooded in. It was a serenely pleasant space, or so I thought.

I went in every day that week and got to grips with the work. The first week went well. I met with every member of the team, understood their frustrations, key challenges and a number of barriers. It was up to me to turn those into opportunities. That was, after all, why they had engaged me.

One day, after an avocado and bacon sandwich on brown flatbread, I poured myself a coffee, in my office. While reviewing some papers, there was a knock on the door.

I heard a stifled voice, say, "Vivika, General Salim is on the line for you."

"Put him through please, Sophie," I said.

Sophie went back to her office and put me through to Boss- Man.

"It's me," he said.

"Excuse me, who?" I asked. I was simply not going to play his game. And though he was a memorable character, an owner, an investor, a big shot, I was not going to entertain it without pushback.

"This is General Salim Karim Ali bin Saeed Al Achbari al Taeni," he barked.

"Ah. General Salim. How are you, Your Excellency? I am sincerely sorry for your loss."

"Thank you," he said.

"Ms Vivika, you are the new person in charge of sales and marketing, are you not?"

"I am, indeed, Sir," I answered.

"Listen here," he said. "Your company has made a tremendous hash-up of this entire collaboration. I am hoping that you will be the one rational brain who may see sense and get us out of this incredible pit. I am frustrated beyond words. I am pulling my hair out, not that I have much left, and whatever remains, I like to keep short. But that is beside the point. I am at the end of my tether."

He shouted something or other in Arabic to someone in his office, and then continued,

"What are you, and when I say you, I mean you specifically, going to do about this?

Your predecessors, long gone, kept hiding behind their teams, rather than taking the lead and being accountable for their actions. I assume you are qualified, capable, experienced, resourceful, and committed. So, what is it that you are going to do? Or are you going to give me excuses too? Beautiful words and a load of utter bull? I am an engineer and a mathematician. I work on facts, not fantasies. And I am not at all satisfied." He sounded angry now.

"The company you are working for have let me down," he continued. "They sold me stories. They are totally and utterly, I repeat, completely and undeniably, rubbish, inept and incompetent. So, once again, I ask you, what are you going to do?"

I was about to say something when he went on.

"I planned to open up projects in Egypt proper, on the Sinai peninsula, Oman, Kenya, Ras al Khaimah and other countries, and what do I get? Incompetence. Excuses. A load of nonsense. If I weren't well-educated, I would be more explicit, but for your sake and mine, I shall not slide into foul language, although only those words fully describe the dross and derelict company you joined.

I am genuinely sorry that you were not aware of who or what you have let yourself in with, though you will no doubt soon realise the error of your ways.

What do you have to say for yourself? What do you plan to do? Hmm?"

Then he was silent. He was clearly waiting for my response. I said, "Sir, I fully appreciate your frustration. Please allow me to set out the challenges and, at the same time, offer opportunities that will mitigate barriers, grow business, and enhance solutions. I do realise that may sound like "management speech", but please allow me three working days to revert to you and present the relevant, achievable, and measurable plan going forward. With your input, the strategy will be aligned and implemented. We shall review every two weeks what the progress is and what needs re-aligning or which policies are not working well and need adjusting to reach our objectives that we mutually agree upon from the onset. Is that agreeable to you, Your Excellency?"

Silence.

Followed by, "*Ya Rabbi*. Oh, my Lord. Hallelujah! Finally, I have found someone in this company who listens and can communicate. I am most pleased to have spoken to you. Welcome aboard, and you must be back in the Middle East very soon. Next week it will be. I will clear my diary and advise the CEO."

With that, he rang off and was gone.

What a whirlwind this guy is, I thought. He is hard-working, demanding, highly professional and determined, but Lord help us if he becomes part of my Every Day.

I followed up with General Salim with a concise email. A pragmatic approach. Clear cut. Straight talking.

He told me he was an engineer and a mathematician and that he communicated in facts.

And that is what I did. I recapped our conversation. I highlighted some findings, conclusions and recommendations and spoke in precise and exact terms.

I re-read the message briefly and pressed "send".

I was reflecting on the conversation when there was a knock on the door of my office.

Four of the team spilt into my office, asking, "What did he say?"

Sophie asked, "Did he give you a hard time? He can be so nasty."

Jennifer jumped in, saying "We are so sorry, we could not

evade the call. Poor you. Baptism by fire. Can we make you a cup of tea? We got organic blueberry tarts from next door. They are crazy delicious. We saved you one."

"General Salim is such a horrible man," Sophie said. "Yes, he is wealthy, well-respected and prominent in his part of the world.

But with us, he always gives us a hard time. We truly don't like that man at all. He makes us feel like we are totally incompetent. He orders us around like we are in some platoon."

I realised General Salim was feared by the people in office. And indeed, he had been outrageously outspoken during the team meeting in Dubai.

A bit of a bully, really. On reflection, however, to be fair, Boss- Man had a point. A very valid one. His investments were in the hundreds of millions of dollars, and seriously, you would expect a capable company to be doing a great job. However, that, from General Salim's perspective, did not appear to be the case.

I had worked in international hospitality for many years and could see significant cracks and gaps in this organisation, from the moment I joined. It was worrying, and I was not sure what could be done to fix things, especially with big egos and prima-donnas at the helm.

I did not think General Salim was incompetent. Callous and explosive, yes. But incompetent, definitely not.

After a tea-break with the team, I returned to my office to find an email with General Salim's c.v. in my inbox. *How weird*, I thought. *Why did he send me that?*

Your Excellency

The following morning, I opened General Salim's email from the evening before.

It read, "Salim here. Book a flight. I need to discuss strategy with you. Tell useless Redhead I insisted you meet me. Be here by Tuesday. Send flight details. Regards".

"Bollocks," I said out loud. Whatever next?

I guess I had best contact Shannon, who was, after all, my boss. I was about to call her when my phone rang. It was "Redhead".

No coincidence. Of that, I was sure. "Hi, Shannon, good morning."

"Hi, Vivika. Hope all is well." She did not wait for my response and continued, "You need to go to Oman on Monday night and attend a meeting with His Excellency, General Salim on Tuesday. I cannot make it, but you must. If you have anything else in the diary, please cancel all and book your flight back on Saturday but be flexible if needed. You don't need a visa before you fly. You can get it at the airport, and anyway, all will be arranged. Sophie will take care of matters and liaise with General Salim's PA. Please note to keep Zeina, his PA, firmly on your side. She is his right hand and has been with him for seventeen years now. Not an easy feat if you ask me, but it is not for me to judge.

Please keep me up to date daily on his feedback and conversations. His properties are crucial to our brand and portfolio, and without him, we have no product or business. You seem to have struck a chord with him, so go. When he says jump, we say, how high? Any questions?"

"No, I can't think of any," I replied.

"Very good. That is settled then. Safe flight." And with that, Shannon hung up and was gone.

That seemed to be the format. Deliver a big message and move on.

When Boss-Man says jump, everybody says, "How high?". *How ridiculous.* I thought. Anyhow, I did not have a choice and frankly, I had nothing to lose. I decided to go with the flow and do the best I could to deliver.

In the office that morning, I called my PA.

"Sophie, good morning. I hope all is well. Please can you book me a flight?" I said.

"I have it here already," she replied. Ms Efficiency, PA to the Über-Power of the Middle East, General Salim, had already arranged everything.

Taking no for an answer was never on the cards. What he said appeared to go.

I was personally not at all OK with that. I didn't appreciate being controlled.

We landed in Oman.

While I was waiting for my suitcase, I noticed a young man coming towards me.

"Ms Vivika, welcome to Oman. I have your visa. Allow me to secure your luggage, and I will take you to the Serrengi Che Muscat for you to check-in."

His English was immaculate. His tone was friendly and professional.

"Thank you," I said, "What is your name?" I asked.

"Mustafa," the young man replied.

His primrose yellow and purple turban was knotted most attractively around his handsome head. He must have been in his early twenties, tall and smiling. A proud Omani.

"His Excellency, General Salim will join you for dinner tonight at eight," Mustafa said. "You will find instructions in your room," he added.

Somehow, the fact that I would have to follow instructions came as no surprise to me. *Let me see how I will be able to handle Boss-Man*, I thought.

The reception area was like a Bedouin Tent. Intricate lanterns with vanilla coloured candles, gave the place a gentle golden flickering glow, while casting geometric Arabesque patterns on the plastered walls and green slate floor.

Mini palm trees were placed in sand-coloured oversized pots, under the dome of the "tent", which was open to the night sky. It was done with great taste and style, I considered, like in the 1001 Arabian Nights.

Somebody had given the Reception Experience a lot of thought. *Perhaps a stage director had been hired to seamlessly put this moving composition together*. It was enchanting.

The hotel was surrounded by lush gardens, interspersed with jetting water fountains and the shimmering Arabian Sea beyond. It felt like an utter slice of heaven. I was privileged and excited to be there.

My "room" turned out to be a spacious modern bungalow, almost like a glass cube. It had a lovely courtyard garden, with bright orange and cyclamen-coloured *Majnooneh*, growing up the outside walls. The literal translation of Clematis, in Arabic, is "crazy one". The climbing plant grows everywhere, adding vibrant shades to any garden or courtyard. I also noticed large shrubs of mint, lavender, and honeysuckle. Due to the amount of glass, which you were able to tint at the press of a button, the transition between accommodation and garden was seamless.

In the bathroom suite was a large square sunken granite bath. It was filled to the brim with hot water, freshly run by someone, probably on my arrival at check-in.

The amenities in the suite were oversized. The same went for the "mini"-bar.

Each exquisite decanter had its own Omani silver necklace, placed around its neck. Whisky, Cognac and Pimm's No.1. *Pimm's in Oman?* I found it surprising and fabulous.

I poured myself a tumbler, added a strawberry, cucumber peel and ginger ale, along with plenty of cubes from the ice bucket. It felt nice to be back in the lap of luxury, and back in the Middle East. The Mystical Middle East, where things were never quite what they seemed. Smoke and mirrors. And where anything could happen.

I slipped out of my clothes and into the tub, together with my Pimm's.

After a lovely soak, I dried myself and wore the bathrobe.

I settled in for a snooze which turned into a glorious and heavy sleep. Profoundly relaxed and hardly able to move, I re-emerged after some hours. Dusk was setting in.

I opened the sliding patio doors. The honeysuckle scent wafted in.

Life is perfect, I thought.

I filled up my marble sink with cold water and added the rest of the ice cubes from my ice bucket. I splashed my face, my breasts, my arms, and body.

Refreshed, I opened my case and saw that my clothes were wrinkled.

I whipped out the iron and ironing board, fixed a coffee, and picked out a chic pair of linen trousers and a relaxed-fitting tunic with a tempting tassel. Classy yet casual. I wore my small, simple gold hoop earrings, one with a pearl, the other with a small Mayan pendant from Guatemala, making the outfit finished yet personalised, just as I liked it.

I sprayed on some fragrance, then applied some light make-up and scooped my hair up in a loose ponytail. I was now ready to meet Boss-Man.

I refused to make too much of an effort. *Why would I?*

Having heard a rustling sound, I noticed a note being slid under my door.

The message simply read, "Meeting place is at the Lobster Shack on the Beach at 8 o'clock".

The handwritten note was neat but had no name or signature. It went on to say, "It will take you eight minutes to walk there, or you can order a cart".

I slipped into my gem-studded flip flops and headed off to the beach in the dark. I left the room at ten minutes to eight o'clock, to arrive at the restaurant on time.

Torches surrounded "The Shack".

There were benches carved into the sand, like sunken sit-pits, with oversized plumped-up colourful cushions and bonfires separating each private area.

I spotted Boss-Man immediately. He stood near a generously sized table for two, set slightly apart from the boardwalk leading to the Shack. I walked towards him, as he approached me.

"Good evening, young lady," he said in a firm voice.

"Good evening, Your Excellency," I said as I stretched out my hand to greet him.

He did not reach out to shake mine. Instead, he put his right hand over his heart. I was confused but recovered quickly and put my hand down without shaking his.

He invited me over to the table.

"I prefer not to sit in the sand today and have arranged for an alternative. I hope that meets with your approval," General Salim said.

I smiled and nodded politely.

The Restaurant Manager and an army of waiters were hovering in the background, clearly on stand-by.

General Salim asked me about my flight and what I would like to drink. It was a welcome offer.

"Opus One?" he quipped.

I had no idea what he was talking about. I know that "Opus" means "work" in Latin.

I recalled it from my Latin classes many years ago. But what "work", was General Salim referring to? A concert? An opera? He clocked my confusion and summoned the Maître d', standing by, saying,

"The young lady would like a glass of Opus One. I will join her. Bring a bottle."

"Certainly, Sir." The Maître d' knew the *Spiel*. Bring what is needed, keep the owner happy and stay out of sight. Be discreet while always being on hand.

"So," General Salim began. "When we spoke last week, after the conversation we had, if you recall, I sent you my c.v."

"Yes," I said, "Thank you. I was interested to learn you were educated in the UK. How did you enjoy living there?"

General Salim did not respond and said, "But I never received yours. And that surprised me. Because if I send you my bio., I would at least expect to receive yours."

Embarrassed and trying to think on my feet, I could only stutter, "I will send it to you as soon as I can. I am very sorry. I did not think my c.v. was of importance to you."

"It is," he said. "I am interested to know who is supposed to be turning my fortune around. And if it is up to you, then I certainly want to know "All About You"."

As I looked at him across the table, the flicker of the torches that surrounded the place flashed across his chiselled face. I caught a glimpse of something I could not quite place, reflected in his coal-black eyes.

Confused, I looked away. Boss-Man did not.

Thankfully the food arrived, which was utterly delicious. But above all, its arrival was very timely.

After an awkward start, I could see that Boss-Man was well trained in making anyone feel comfortable, should he choose to do so. He made sure I knew that he had the power to ruffle my feathers. General Salim then proceeded to prove that he could equally relax me and put me at ease.

Opus One, when it arrived, turned out to be an exquisite tasting, robust red wine.

Boss-Man looked at the year. "I am glad you saved me a vintage year, Alain," he said to the sommelier. Turning to me, he said, "This is one of the most exceptional vintages Opus One ever produced. Dark fruit and velvet tannins, with a hint of oak. Its complexity will most likely continue to grow over the next thirty years or so, which, if I am not mistaken is around your age, isn't it? Around thirty-five?" Without stopping for me to affirm or correct his statement, he continued, "As for the food to go with the wine, I recommend the steak. Saignant. Rare. It is essential to have it served precisely right with the juices oozing and optimising the flavours of the exquisite Wagyu."

I couldn't help feeling an underlying message in his dark voice as he spoke the words. It made me think of Hélène, when she had dinner that time with Michel, on her first night in Jordan. I smiled, thinking that "steak, juices and innuendos", clearly transcend borders in the Middle East.

Dinner was exquisite.

Boss-Man settled down into exciting conversations about trips to Africa, his investments in various parts of the world and his travels as a youngster.

He talked about the region and the change that occurred when the oil was discovered. Suddenly, General Salim stopped in mid-pepper-grind. He looked up at me and smiled.

"This song, by that brilliant vocal group Boney M.," he said, his eyes glistening in the candlelight, "was released at the very time when we went from desert to disco and exchanged our life for glam and glitter."

There was an air of nostalgia when he said it.

I wasn't quite sure how to interpret it. But what I felt was an emotion, a moment of reminiscence, which somehow made me warm a little bit to this man, who I had firmly fixed in my mind as being obnoxious and cold-hearted.

I quickly recovered from letting my guard down.

Though General Salim could clearly be utterly charming, it seemed he was manipulating my response to him. By interjecting some humanity and humour, his aim was probably to give me a false sense of security and then knock me right off balance again.

The rest of the dinner was pleasant, and we talked a bit about work but not a lot.

After dinner, two golf carts were made available, one to take me to my room and the other to drop General Salim.

Before parting ways, General Salim said his driver would pick me up at nine o'clock in the morning. He informed me that we would meet at his Muscat Office. He wished me good night, and I was driven back to "my place".

I took a quick shower and considered the day, which had been pretty good.

The meeting with Boss-Man, all in all, had been OK. The food, wine and setting certainly had been spectacular. And he had behaved like a gentleman.

Perhaps he was not all bad and, at least partly, human after all.

Ali Baba

I woke up to the phone ringing and answered it.

"Ms Vivika, I have Ali Baba on the line for you," the person on the other end of the phone said.

"Ali Baba?" I muttered.

Confused, I was about to say there must be some sort of mistake, but the gentle voice said, "Connecting you now."

"Good morning, Ms Vivika. Ali Baba here. How are you on this bright and sunny morning?"

Perplexed, I realised it was Boss-Man. I quickly recovered and said, "Good morning, General Salim."

"Ali Baba is my pseudonym. Otherwise, they may ask questions before putting me through."

He laughed. He sounded fresh and upbeat and boyishly proud of his astute prank on the telephone operator.

"Ah!" I could hear his smile in his voice. "It seems I woke you up, young lady. Do you think you are on holiday, rather than getting ready to discuss strategy?"

I cleared my voice. I was mortified, as General Salim was right, he had woken me.

At the same time, I was embarrassed as I didn't know what to say.

"How did you sleep?" he went on to ask.

"Very well, thank you, General Salim. All was wonderful, and I am most grateful for everything."

"Never mind about all that," he said. "Get yourself up, have a decent breakfast and make sure you are in the main entrance by nine o'clock, as agreed. I will see you in my office. I am off to a meeting and will be back by then."

With that, he left me hanging, the flat line still buzzing in my ear.

Jeez. Bugger. Bollocks. I can't believe this man. This is crazy. Why even call when we already had an agreement and a set time to meet? Just to ensure he could unsettle my day from the moment I open my eyes? What sort of day will this be? How annoying. Anyhow, I thought to myself, *I better get up and jump under the shower. And not let this bother me.*

Mustafa, who had dropped me the day before, greeted me politely and gave me a charming smile. He opened my door, and I stepped into the same BMW 7 series in which he had picked me up the previous day. Or, perhaps not, I realised.

This car's interior had a different coloured trim around the cream leather seats.

Silly me. Of course, General Salim has a fleet of BMW's, not just the one.

It was already hot at nine o'clock in the morning.

I wore dark blue flared linen trousers, a pair of cream-coloured wedges and a silk cream top. I left my hair loose. I brought my hand-embroidered pashmina with me.

It was gifted to me by my girlfriend who used to live in

Oman. She had given me this exquisite item that I loved and took everywhere with me. It had purples and lavenders, with flecks of gold and was adorned with some beautiful champagne-coloured beads.

It seemed appropriate that it originated from Oman and was now back where it came from. I was happy that had I rolled it up in my tote, on stand-by, for whenever I felt I needed moral support, almost like a comfort blanket.

I arrived in the cold central hall of the office building.

I draped my pashmina loosely around my shoulders. Mustafa pressed the button to call the elevator, which took us, uninterrupted, to the penthouse floor.

When I stepped out of the lift, Ms Efficiency, the PA of General Salim, came to greet me. "*Ahlan wa sahlan*. Welcome," she smiled.

"I hope you were comfortable and had a good night's sleep."

"Yes, thank you very much," I said, "All was great."

"Please have a seat," she said. "I will send for coffee."

An older gentleman of Asian descent arrived minutes later and offered me a small cup of coffee and some ice water. I thanked him and looked around. On the stark white walls, there were some colourful pictures, hand-painted, I think. Some of them looked like they could have been a Degas or a Monet.

I didn't consider until much later that perhaps they were the genuine article.

"Ding".

The lift door opened and into the penthouse office skated Boss-Man.

He walked at speed and with purpose. "Ms Vivika. Good

morning and welcome."

His jovial tone of the morning had made way for a more solemn and authoritarian one.

"I shall be with you in a minute... Zeina," he yelled with a booming voice.

Ms Efficiency came running in. "Yes, Your Excellency?"

"Bring me my papers, hold my calls and book dinner for me. You know where."

"Certainly, General Salim," she replied and sped off.

He turned to me, saying, "Now then, come on through to the board room."

He held out his hand to shake mine. Utterly confused, I shook it.

Then he stepped back and gallantly gave way for me to enter the board room before him.

He once again unsettled me. *Why decline to shake my hand last time when we met for dinner, but invite me to shake his hand on this occasion?*

"Take a seat," he said.

The long oval table was made of beautiful wood. It looked like it was regularly and lovingly polished. The piece stood like a magnificent *objet d'art*, in the middle of the commanding space.

The views from the board room were spectacular.

From the large windows, I admired the mystical Omani mountains, that surrounded Muscat. There was no high-rise to speak of. We were the highest tower.

I later learned that Damsonite Properties' building was the highest building in the entire Sultanate.

"Now then, young lady, what did you prepare to show me?"

General Salim said.

I thought I could not have heard him right.

"Excuse me?" I said.

"What did you want to show me?" he repeated.

I felt the blood run to my cheeks. My legs felt weak. I looked at General Salim, not sure what to say.

He said, "You came all this way without wanting to show me anything?"

Then he shot me an utterly unexpected and bedazzling grin and embarrassed me further by saying, "I am sure next time you will have something you will give me, but for today, let me explain what I expect and what I need from you."

He pressed a button on the intercom and bellowed, "Zeina! Papers!"

Ms Efficiency came in, walking fast but keeping her professional cool. She placed three different piles on the boardroom table in front of General Salim.

A USB was slotted into the laptop which had been on the boardroom table all along.

The electric wiring disappeared seamlessly through the table into a hidden socket beneath the camel-coloured carpet. Everything was arranged with precision.

"Connect the presentation, so we can begin," he instructed Zeina.

"And have AJ bring me my coffee and ensure Ms Vivika has some of that juice from the farm."

Then turning to me, he said, "AJ has been with me for twenty-six years. His son works for me too."

A random bit of information, but none the less a small insight, relating to the man in the room.

The presentation on the screen behind him started. He paused it.

"Are you ready?" he asked, locking his eyes on to mine. That look again.

I looked back at him. "I am," I said.

He nodded as if I had given my agreement to something much more significant than watching the presentation. "Then let us proceed," he said, and he pressed "play".

O.G.S.Ms

General Salim showed me the projects that were under construction, across three continents, and in twelve different locations. They were all grand-scale developments and incorporated a university, two hospitals, a mixed-use development with a theme park, multiple apartments, office buildings and an art gallery.

General Salim said, "We take the best from the Germans, and from the Brits. We collaborate closely with the Dutch, as they are among the very best." His insinuation was not lost on me.

I managed to continue my notes and focused on areas relevant to my work.

On the subject of profit and loss, I wanted to learn where we were winning, where we were losing. What the gaps were. Once I understood that, we could discuss our goals and ensure we had a plan. Having spent the past few hours discussing multiple topics, I wanted to understand more about the strategic plan, and method used.

"Do you have the OGSM plan?" I asked.

"OGSM?" he questioned.

His energy shifted; his physique changed. His face was ironically quizzical.

"I have not yet seen any plan provided by your organisation, that would give me the pleasure of an exquisite OGSM, but perhaps you are about to change all that."

I blushed at the intended suggestive reference to orgasm.

I was halfway through explaining that OGSMs related to business planning through Objectives, Goals, Strategies and Measures when he interrupted me and smiled.

"Don't worry," he said, "We own several Fortune500 companies all over the world. They all have OGSMs. I am glad to hear we are on the same page, and that OGSMs are what guide us and keep us on track."

General Salim got up from his chair and said, "Excuse me, nature calls."

He disappeared through a door that led out from the board room and came back sometime later.

He looked washed, refreshed. The fragrance of Oud was more pronounced now.

I was not complaining. I could get lost in that scent whoever wore it.

"Time for lunch," he proclaimed. "We will have it in the office and finish up what we need to do."

Then, without any warning, he bellowed, "Zeina!"

Like a genie, Zeina, re-appeared with AJ. Zeina laid the far end of the board-room table.

Freshly prepared tabbouleh, scattered with pomegranate seeds, mixed with sliced black olives, as well as some home-made humous and freshly baked Arabic flat-bread which was still warm. Stuffed aubergine, with walnuts and peppers, called *makdous*, and a large jug of freshly prepared lemon and mint juice, graced the table.

Afterwards, we cleansed our palate with slices of fresh peach and watermelon. The Arabic version of tapas, I thought. I found the mezze delicious and light. Afterwards AJ offered us hot towel to wash our hands and a cold one to refresh our face. I asked to go to the loo before we started the meeting again.

"You can use my bathroom if you don't mind. It is just through there."

General Salim pointed to the door through which he had disappeared before lunch.

As I got up, Zeina's voice came through the intercom.

"Your Excellency, I cannot keep your wife on hold any longer. She insists she needs to speak with you."

I heard General Salim taking the call, saying, "*Salam wa Alaikum*,", which translates as "peace be upon you" which I realised was a regular greeting. I heard it before.

I then entered the bathroom as the conversation continued in Arabic.

I wondered what General Salim's wife would be like and whether he was married to more than one woman. *Did he have children? What would he be like as a husband and a father?* The lights came on automatically as I entered the bathroom. It was a large space, equipped with a full shower, a loo, a towel rack, and large bottles of expensive fragrances, including an unusual, beautiful black one. Written in what looked like Arabic calligraphy, a single word had been painted on, in what looked like liquid gold.

I had no idea what it said. I knew the Arabic script read

from right to left, but I, naturally, was unable to decipher what was written.

I took the bottle and lifted the glass stopper from its position. Out danced the scent of Oud. The fragrance of a Caliph, a King, a Sultan. The hallmark of an Arabian royal hunter, in pursuit of his prey.

I inhaled deeply. Oh, Lord. How utterly intoxicating.

I freshened up and came back out. My spirit had changed. General Salim was still on the phone. As I entered, he looked up at me without much ado, though somehow, he sniffed the shift in me.

General Salim did not gesture me to sit down, so I inspected the art on the walls until he hung up. I was aware that I was acting like a slightly frazzled bird, which was not sure whether to perch and rest or take flight and escape.

"Well, Miss Vivika, I have spent more time with you than I do with my board members. The time has come for me to start the next part of my day and evening. I have three functions and have an *aza* to attend."

Seeing that I didn't quite understand what an *aza* was, he explained that this is the gathering after someone has passed away and is the opportunity for family, friends and acquaintances to offer their sympathies and condolences.

"The *aza* takes place over three days and today is the last day to attend, so I am compelled to go. It can be a pain in the neck with all these people dying," he said, "but not as tedious as those elaborate weddings with a thousand people as a minimum. That number is considered small in our books. Luckily, I am usually in London and the South of France over the summer as that is the time that most weddings take place."

I perked up when he said he would be in London.

This well-spoken, British-sounding Arab man was intriguing. I wondered whether he would also wear his sheet, his dish-dash?

Maybe I would see him there some day, in European clothing. How different would that be? I wondered.

As if reading my thoughts, he said, "Of course you will see me in London. We are opening a property not far from there. I put in an offer on a country house just outside Oxford. Such a great place," he went on.

"Maybe it is the university memories that keep me coming back. Or the fact that I dated this lovely British girl, Rachel, for some years. My being there evokes my romantic side, perhaps. I enjoy going back for more of the same. I can never get enough of it."

More innuendo. This man had some experience with women and knew how to play this game.

"Ms Vivika, If you don't mind me saying so, you look hot." That gentle sardonic smile again.

"Why don't you take off that lovely pashmina, that makes your eyes look like lavender in spring. You can then allow yourself to cool down and show off some of that cream you are sporting underneath."

Was he talking about my cream top or my cream skin underneath my top?

My cheeks were on fire, and my neck felt hot. I hate it that I go blotchy when I am embarrassed.

I could not do anything apart from slip off my pashmina. I gulped the water from the glass in front of me.

How could anybody be so obvious yet so subtle, so provocative, yet appear polite and concerned with my welfare?

General Salim was relaxed and said, "Mind if I smoke?"

He did not wait for my reply as he slid his Cohiba cigar out of its bright yellow holster. The top third of the tube was covered with tiny black and white squares, like a mosaic.

I could imagine making a chandelier if I had around a hundred of them. Perhaps I should stick to one and carry my tampons around in it. Elegant, original, subtle, and individual. I liked the idea.

Boss-Man was watching me and said, "Seems you like my holster. Have it if it satisfies you. If not, I will chuck it out."

He rolled the now empty cigar tube towards me, across the table.

I picked it up and slid it into my bag on the chair next to me, giving him a small smile of appreciation mixed with an appropriate dose of defiance.

He read me seamlessly, his nostrils flaring momentarily. "I think this is enough for one day," he said.

"Mustafa will drop you back at the hotel. There is an event taking place on the beach tonight with an astronomer and a group of people from Europe. I wouldn't normally know about these things, but I asked Zeina to find out what is going on at the resort, to keep you busy, usefully engaged and entertained until we meet up later. See if you can help out. I will meet you for dinner."

Once again, he raised his voice, pressed the button on the device and shouted, "Zeina!"

"Yes, Your Excellency." Zeina's voice came through the intercom.

"Arrange for Ms Vivika to be dropped off. We are done."

And with a click, Zeina was instantly both muted and dismissed.

Turning to me, he said, "Ms Vivika, having spent a good part of the day together, how do you feel about making this work?"

I knew he was playing with words and said, "I know what needs to be done, and it will be achieved," followed by a confident and bright smile.

"I am impressed with your ability, your energy, your experience and your original thoughts. I also think you are not as full of bull as the Redhead, who calls herself your superior. She is not. The opposite is true. I hope you practice what you preach, Ms Vivika.

As we all know, words without actions are merely hot air. Do you rely on hot air, Ms Vivi, to make your balloon fly?"

"Ms. Vivi". Nobody ever called me that. Vivi yes, but the formal and the informal blended together, by someone I did not know, threw me off. Professional and somehow intimate.

Intimidating, I thought, *but not entirely unpleasant.*

Zeina walked in.

"Mustafa is waiting for you," she said and smiled politely. I detected a level of ownership over General Salim.

I was a visiting female and spent a good number of hours in General Salim's den.

On his turf, with no one else present.

She probably knew him well. I was certainly not the first sales and marketing girl he had sold his charms to, nor would I be the last. The thought struck me, *Was I buying?*

"Shannon asked me to tell you to call her just as soon as you get to your hotel," Zeina said.

More instructions. This time from the assistant of Boss-Man. Wow, I was getting it from all directions.

"By the way," Boss-Man said, "you will be going off to one of my new resorts in the Maldives, not a million miles from here.

I want you to inspect the place and let me know whether you think I should affiliate it with your group.

I will rely on your insights and feedback. Your CEO has been trying to persuade me most ineffectively to secure it under your company flag. So far, I have refused, as I have not been impressed. However, in your small and relatively insignificant tenure to date, Ms Vivika, you have managed to rouse my interest. Quite significantly so.

As a direct result, I may consider letting you market this very upscale property.

You will go there tomorrow night, arriving early the following morning and returning to me on Saturday."

He never asked me. He simply told me. I am due to fly back on Saturday. Then I remembered what Shannon said.

"You are flying back on Saturday unless General Salim decides differently. And if he says "jump", we from our side say "how high?"."

I recovered and said that whatever was needed to support both his investments and the name of the group, I was ready to do.

Then I asked, "Would you please ensure that my boss knows my movements and can agree accordingly?"

"I do not ask for permission, Ms Vivika. They report to me, not the other way around. Instructions have already been sent." Now my head was swirling; I could not make head nor tail of the communication that must have gone on between Boss-Man, Ms Efficiency, Redhead and, no doubt, the CEO too. It was clear who was in charge.

Toes in the Sand

That night, I was introduced to Dominic, the director of
events at the hotel.

"Nice to meet you, Ms Vivika. We have heard great things
about you. We understand that your expertise has been offered
to support us with our event on the beach tonight, and we
are most grateful for any insights and ideas. Please meet me
at "Bedu Beach Bar" at seven o'clock. We can then review the
setup." I was there on the dot of seven and met Dominic.

He told me about the astronomer who would be entertaining
some twenty guests on the beach, for a stargazing session. It
sounded lovely. While it was a good basic set up, I just thought
some unique details were missing.

I asked Dominic if they had some simple brown paper bags
that we could fill with sand, in which we could place a candle
and light it. The effect of the gentle flickering glow in these
paper brown bags is so organic and beautiful that it completes
most any setting, whether rustic or chic. I felt that it would
transform the scene on the beach.

The barman was sent to get me some bags. I took them and

cut patterns so that the candlelight could shine through.

As I was cutting and sticking, I got hungry and ordered a seafood salad and a glass of Chablis.

It took quite some time to finish my creative interpretations.

The guests weren't due until eleven o'clock at night, so I was OK to take my time.

Cuttings, folded paper, scissors, and glue dotted the table.

Amongst the handicraft debris were my salad and chilled white wine.

Suddenly, I heard that voice. My heart skipped a beat. "Well, good evening, Ms Vivi. Aren't you the artist?"

I looked up. There was General Salim, in the most pristine dish-dash, standing right by my side and looking down on me.

How disturbing, I thought, noting that I was pleased to see him.

"Would you join me for dinner?" he asked.

"I can't," I replied. "I need to finish cutting these patterns, and I need to do that before the guests show up."

He looked at me and said, "You need dinner."

"Thank you, General Salim, but I had a bite to eat while I was doing the bags."

He looked at me more intently and said, "I thought I was going to have dinner with you this evening. Was that not what we agreed in my office this morning?"

"I got hungry," I said, quickly adding, "Thank you for your kind offer."

"Well, it seems that I best get changed and wait for you to finish. Come and find me when you have delivered what you committed to."

He suppressed a smile and went.

I continued and finished my work. Pleased with the result, Dominic and I placed them around the telescope on the beach. The setting was complete.

Dominic and I double high-fived each other and went our separate ways.

As I walked up to the main building, I found Boss-Man sitting with two European women, having a drink. He had not changed his dish-dash. Clearly, he was waylaid *en route*.

The women, who were mature professionals, but very "well kept", shall we say, were openly flirting with Boss-Man.

Power is sexy to some, I guess. It intrigued me to see the way they played with their coiffed locks and the way they reeled with laughter at General Salim's remarks.

As I walked by, General Salim made it quite clear what was going to happen next.

"You may have dined without me, but we need to discuss some matters. So, please join me." It was not a request. More like a veiled order.

General Salim excused himself to the ladies, who looked bemused. He made it clear I was expected to follow him.

General Salim escorted me to a seating area, set back from the main terrace.

Boss-Man settled in on one side of the table on a comfortable bench. I sat opposite him, on the other, sand underfoot.

He ordered a bottle of red without asking me. I was happy with whatever.

He told me that the two women he was sitting with were his European PR arm and that I should meet with them when back in London.

We settled reasonably quickly into a conversation. I learned

General Salim had five children, including identical twins.

Once again, General Salim voiced his frustration with the group I worked for. At some stage, the conversation got heated, though not hostile.

I disagreed on a point he made and decided to take him on.

He was an intelligent man and excellent at both conversation and light-hearted banter.

Having refilled my glass of wine, he leaned side-ways and peered underneath the table.

I did not know why he was looking, but ducked under too, to see what he was observing He straightened back up and laughed, with a twinkle in his eye.

"What?" I exclaimed. "What is so funny?"

I looked under the table to see what had amused him, but could not see why.

He smiled and said, "Why, Ms Vivika. Do you always throw off what you are wearing when you get animated?"

There I was, in my bare feet, with my toes in the sand.

"You tease," I whispered under my breath.

"Ms Vivika, the word *teez*, is Arabic slang for the part of the body that you sit on. And your *teez*, is exceptional, if I may say so."

"Inappropriate," I quipped. "but you know that."

He gave me a wink and said, "No offence intended."

"None taken," I said and winked right back at him. His eyes lit up. Then he poured the rest of the wine.

Twenty minutes later, he offered to take me to my room in his golf cart, which I graciously accepted.

When we arrived, he stopped in front of the steps of my impressive chalet.

"Good night, General Salim," I said.

Without a second thought, I leant over, kissed him on both cheeks, and slid off the passenger seat.

He looked slightly taken aback but recovered quickly.

Was my bold manner too European, I wondered? *Never mind,* I thought. *That is what I am. European.*

I looked back over my shoulder at him as I reached the door.

With a boyish smile, he said, "Good night, Ms Vivika, sleep well."

He waited until I had closed the front door behind me.

Trouble in Paradise

I was up early and made my way over to the breakfast patio. I enjoyed a leisurely bite and was about to leave the restaurant when there he was. It was so unexpected. When he caught sight of me, he stopped in his tracks, locked his eyes onto mine, and flashed the most hugely confident and flirtatiously enchanting smile I had ever experienced. Involuntarily, I found myself beaming back at him.

Damn. When my body is responding before my brain, there will be trouble in paradise.

After the morning encounter, I kept reliving that moment. It can only have taken seconds, but it was etched in my mind. That flash of a smile. That knowing look brimming with confidence. Such sex-appeal. It was only a few seconds, but the impact of his charismatic gaze on me was undeniable.

Having spent the day at the resort, where I took the time to meet with the PR ladies from London, who were excellent value and hugely entertaining, I went to the mall to pick up a few bits and bobs before the night flight to the Maldives.

I arrived at Male airport at dawn.

There were many early flight arrivals. We all poured into the basic-looking airport which did not feature any air-conditioning to speak of. Here and there, some random fans were rigged up, and several men in uniform stood around smoking and talking to each other.

I was queuing up for passport control when my phone rang. It was General Salim.

"Good morning, Sunshine," he said. "You called me; is everything OK?"

Taken aback, I stumbled, "I did? If I did, it was in error".

I was mortified. "I am so sorry," I said, "When you gave me your number yesterday before I travelled, I put it on my phone, but it must have rung by itself. I didn't mean to ring. It was a pocket call. I am so sorry to have disturbed you at this hour." "No trouble," he said. "You woke me, and I am glad you are safely on the ground. It is a pleasure to start the day by hearing your voice."

He said, "When you get to my resort, send me your room number."

Then, just like that, he was gone.

I cleared passport control and was met on arrival and escorted to the lounge. We waited for the dedicated plane to take us to the resort.

The experience was like travelling back in time. Everything was very laid back and without any stress whatsoever. Rather lovely, it must be said.

Having boarded the bright, scarlet-coloured seaplane, we flew for around forty minutes and landed on the lagoon, alongside a pristine white beach.

We disembarked onto a wooden pier.

The General Manager, Jonno, was there to greet the guests, and me in particular. After all, I was sent by Boss-Man, so he better make sure all my reports would be positive, or so I figured out over the time of my stay.

My house on stilts, built over the water, was oriented towards sunset.

I hugely enjoyed checking out my villa. It had a water slide from the wooden deck above, straight into the lagoon below. The bath was made of glass, so it appeared you were suspended above the water. The hotel amenities were oversized and generous.

The minibar, just like in Muscat, was not mini in any way. The concept resonated with me.

A fruit basket made of driftwood displayed bright fruits including mangos, papaya, pink and white dragon fruit and tiny bananas. It was such a beautiful composition. It was almost like a sculpture, set off against the turquoise waters that gently sparkled in the sunshine.

I had the use of a coral-coloured bike, with little painted sea turtles decorated everywhere. Over the following days, I saw bikes decorated with birds, whales, dolphins, sharks, snakes, lizards, and geckos. Even the reptiles were portrayed in bright colours and looked friendly and fun.

I decided to enjoy and sample everything. I started by taking a shower after my trip.

I then flung on some clothes and found a note under my door inviting me for a massage and Reiki session. I jumped on my bike and cycled to the Spa for my massage. Afterwards I ate sashimi and shrimp and drank a frozen margarita or two. I knew alcohol and massage didn't really go together, but I wanted to get it all in, so I broke some rules and just enjoyed myself.

But something was lacking. I couldn't quite put my finger on it.

I came back to my spectacular room and noticed a missed call. I then found a text on my mobile that said, "Send me your room number".

It was from General Salim.

I felt a sense of excitement. I replied to his text and sent the number, or rather the name of the villa, "Turtle Nest".

Within minutes, the phone rang.

"Hi, Ali Baba here without the forty thieves, but happy to steal some of your time. How are you doing, Miss Vivi?"

"Good afternoon, Your Excellency. How are you?" I replied, adding "I must say your property is truly spectacular."

He asked me about the journey and my first impressions of the resort, especially how it related to the services and facilities. The conversation flowed smoothly until General Salim said,

"Lucky that I am not there."

I was a bit taken aback, and I asked, "Why is that?"

In a thick voice, he replied, "Because you are there to work and had I been there, I don't think much work would have been done."

My breath stuck in my throat, and my body weakened.

I hoarsely replied, with as much confidence as I could muster, "In that case, it may well be best that you are not here at this time. I have work to do."

I could hear him smiling and could feel his desire from afar. He wished me luck and said, "You need to be back here by Saturday as we have a board meeting. It won't be in Oman but in Abu Dhabi. I will have Zeina make arrangements.

Salam and enjoy," he said. I could hear him smile. Then he hung up.

I tried not to overthink the conversation. General Salim had openly flirted with me.

He had taken the time and made an effort to be in touch. I was not sure what to think.

I had to admit to myself, he managed to rouse my interest.

I decided to check my emails, rather than trying to read too much into the conversation.

Messages from Shannon, the Redhead: "Where are you? I have not heard from you. How are things going? Can't believe he flew you to the Maldives property. Try and get it. We need to secure it."

I responded that all was going well, that we had good discussions and that I would do my best. I continued with my other emails and messages that needed to be dealt with.

I suddenly felt exhausted and decided to sleep off the confusion of that call.

Tomorrow was another day. Perhaps I simply misinterpreted what Boss-Man had said. The reality might have been different from the picture I was building in my mind.

After two days on Turtle Island, with its quirky architecture and sumptuously indulgent experiences, I flew out to Male airport and then onwards to the UAE.

Sun-kissed and glowing, I arrived in Abu Dhabi.

The Saayidat Peninsula resort was the next property I was going to visit, and Boss-Man would be there.

I was picked up by Nasser, the driver, who was waiting for

me at arrivals at Abu Dhabi International. He took me to the resort, which was only around thirty minutes from the airport. Nasser had the key to the house where I was staying and showed me how to operate the lighting system and surround-sound using the installed i-Pad. He explained how to work the electronic entry system and code.

There were refreshments and a cold jug of watermelon juice, with some mint and halloumi cheese on the side, a delicious combination I had not come across before but would remember. I was exploring the five-bedroom house when the phone went. "Vivi, I am meeting you in a few hours. I have a last-minute meeting with the rulers to discuss some matters. I will come over to Saayidat afterwards, around ten o'clock, and pick you up. Make sure you are ready." And then, he hung up.

General Salim did not say where we would be going or what we would be doing.

I took some time to relax and enjoy the bath and spectacular "Mini-Palace".

At ten o'clock, my phone flashed and his message popped up. "I am outside".

I grabbed my purse, sprayed on some "Precious Oud" fragrance, which I bought at the airport and jumped in next to him in the cream-coloured Maserati. "Hey girl," he said and beamed his smile at me. I grinned back at him.

"It is not far," he said.

Three minutes later we pulled up into the horseshoe-shaped drive of a large mansion, just about 100 meters or so from the beach.

"Welcome to my Abu Dhabi Home," he said.

General Salim showed me around the ground floor and then

asked, "Would you like some fruit and wine? I brought a nice bottle with me. The dragon fruit is perfect at the moment."

I nodded, adding, "That would be nice."

"Now then," he said, "let's take a seat near the pool so we can talk and have a bite."

The pool was not Olympic size, but huge by anyone's standards.

Steps that resembled the ones leading into a ballroom led down into the water.

The air was balmy and the stars bright, under the Abu Dhabi sky.

This place was out of town, so there was no real light pollution. The ocean looked mesmerising from the terrace. Gentle lights shone up from inside the pool. Little nightlights dotted the spaces between massive candle pillars, which stood like columns, around the deck. It was magical.

"What a wonderful setting this is," I said, "That gorgeous pool, all turquoise and lit up. It looks so inviting. So totally perfect."

"Would you like to go for a swim?" he asked.

"I don't have my bathing costume with me." I smiled. This was true as it was at the other house.

"Hmm," he pondered as he contemplated the problem, feigning concern.

"Let's have some wine, while we think what can be done about that particular challenge."

He uncorked a delicious bottle of full-bodied red wine. We chatted easily.

After a while, he said, "So how about that swim?"

"I don't have my bikini, Sir, but I told you that already." I laughed.

He said, "You can wear my swimming trunks if you like."

I looked him straight in the eye and said, "I am Dutch. Either I go in naked or not at all."

My quick response hit a chord and engaged him further. "Swim," he said. "Give in to temptation. I will go inside."

I don't know what I was thinking, or not but I said, "OK, you go inside and stay there, and I will go for a swim."

For the first time, I sounded as if I was in charge. I was back to being me and not taking any nonsense from any man.

He smiled and went off, only to return with a selection of large and luxurious bath towels.

"I will make myself scarce," General Salim smiled.

"You do that," I said, and he went inside.

I took my clothes off, popped them on the chair and lowered myself into the slightly warm pool and looked up at the Abu Dhabi sky. It was utterly heavenly. With the water covering every inch of my naked body, I swam a couple of lengths and enjoyed this fantastic experience. It was divine.

After a while, I felt cold in the warm water.

Perhaps the anticipation of what may be to come was making me shiver.

I stopped in my tracks, in mid-swim, for what I was witnessing was Boss-Man, totally naked, in the moonlight, making his way down the steps towards me.

He was perfect.

I stayed where I was. I trod water and shivered. Nerves, I guess.

He waded over towards me and then, when the pool got too deep, he swam a swift crawl and continued to swim beyond me. He did a quick U-turn and cradled me from behind.

He kissed my neck and cupped my breasts while I was faced away from him in the water.

He asked me why I was shivering, and I simply said, I was cold. "Come," he said, as he gently coaxed me through the water towards the steps.

He gallantly got out before me, helped me out and made sure I didn't slip. Then he wrapped me in a large towel and topped up my glass of wine.

"There you go, Missy Vivacious."

He placed a glass cut-crystal bowl, filled with plump black cherries before me, and suggested I took my place on the sun-lounger.

Once I was dry and warmed up, he took my towel off and started to kiss my body.

I gasped and enjoyed his expert touch. He knew what he was doing.

Practice makes perfect, they say, and practice General Salim had had. Plenty of it, I was quite sure.

After a wonderful time of serious making out, he said, "Let us move to my son's bedroom. There it is, just next to the pool, to the right of the courtyard."

I said, "No." I was not going to go and use his son's room to play with him.

He asked, "Do you want to sleep with me?"

I said, "No, I do not."

After a good few hours of frolicking, laughing and enjoying each other, he said, "If we are not going to make love, I guess we will have to concentrate on work."

I smiled at him and said, "I quite agree."

We had a wonderful time. I knew General Salim respected

me for not sleeping with him, but that wasn't the reason for my saying no. I simply did not want to, in the circumstances. Something held me back and stopped me from going all the way.

We gathered our clothes, got dressed and jumped into another car, parked in the driveway. Salim drove me back to my place. On arrival, he came round to my door and opened it. He offered me his hand to help me out. Kissing it, he looked at me and said, "They will serve you breakfast at seven. I will pick you up at eight."

I said goodnight and headed into the house. I chose the room closest to the top of the sweeping staircase. I got undressed and fell into bed.

When I woke up, a selection of croissants, jams, coffee and tea in a thermos, some cheeses, fruits, sliced avocado and a variety of bread were laid out in the salon.

How blissful and considerate, I thought.

Happily, it was only just past seven o'clock, giving me almost an hour before being picked up. I decided to take a skinny dip in the pool, jump under the shower, get dressed, pack my bags, and have breakfast.

At eight o'clock sharp, Salim arrived.

As I opened the front door, a butler came around, seemingly out of nowhere. He took my luggage and placed it in the car. This time, Salim showed up in a big white Toyota with heavily tinted windows, one of those cars, which could master any terrain. Many cars in the UAE have tinted windows. Apparently, the grade of permitted darkness relates to rules around nationality and status.

There is no telling what goes on behind those dark sheets of glass.

Salim greeted me with a big smile and opened the car door for me, having dismissed the butler who had wanted to do so. "You look a treat, young lady. It will be my great pleasure to give you the drive of your life. I wouldn't normally take the wheel myself on such a long journey. However, I thought this was a perfect opportunity to have you all to myself without prying eyes or ears. So, Vivi, it's you and me for the next five hours. It is a blissful thought".

I smiled at him, jumped into the car, and we set off.

We chatted, he flirted outrageously, held my hand, and told me some of his past adventures. I felt so relaxed in his company.

At some stage, I must have dozed off. Salim woke me up just before we arrived.

Any sign of intimacy was gone the minute we got out of the car. High professionalism prevailed. The afternoon was spent meeting tour operators from Asia, and in the evening, I attended a VIP dinner for a familiarisation trip from Europe. I had two more nights before flying home. Salim had to participate in another dinner and said he would meet me afterwards at "my place".

After dinner, I received a text message from Salim. "I am on my way back from the Palace. I cannot wait to taste your juice", the message read.

OMG. My tummy turned. His words were blatant and bold, to put it mildly.

I did not know him properly yet. And this was beyond saucy.

Still, it turned me on. *Jeez, General, you don't hold back.* I smiled.

I took a shower and waited for him to arrive. He knocked on the door and came straight in, a cigarette brandished between his lips. He stubbed it out in the nearest ashtray, exhaled and kissed me.

An instant flame started to burn within me. My response to this man was immediate. He knew.

"Come," he said, holding out his hand as he led me into the private patio area next to the pool. We sat down on the bamboo swing seat.

He put his arm around me and lit another cigarette. We chatted. He stroked my hair, kissed my hand, and fondled my breast.

I was overcome with desire.

"Let's go inside," he said with a thick voice.

He led me up the steps into the bedroom. We settled on to the exquisite sheets.

He took it slow. "You are different tonight," he said.

"What do you mean?" I asked.

"Yesterday you didn't want me. Today I think you do."

"I know," I said. "Today, I do."

With that, he kissed me gently and started teasing me, caressing my neck and gently biting my earlobes. We ended up in a tantalising tangle and had sex.

He never took his eyes off me.

It was wonderful. Familiar somehow.

After we made love, we lay together, sprawled across the sheet. He pulled me close to him, and we lay there easily for a while. Then he got up and had a shower. Still wet, he tossed his dish-dash over his head, looked me in the eyes and said, "That, young lady, was truly memorable."

He then added "We have one more night, tomorrow. I will not see you during the day. I will be at yours at nine o'clock. Have dinner before. You will need it."

With that, he kissed me on the lips, ruffled my hair and left.

Pole Position

Ienjoyed breakfast on my terrace, caught up with emails, dipped in the pool, and wrote postcards.

I then met with the sales team, tried out the saltwater pool, went on a Dhow cruise and swam with the dolphins. But I was just filling in time and waiting for the day to pass. I just wanted to see Salim again.

Finally, that message I had been waiting for; "I am on my way, I need twenty minutes".

I had just come out of the shower. I decided I would put on a bit of make-up first, before getting dressed. I slipped into my bathrobe and settled into drying my hair.

Exactly twenty minutes after I received his text, there was a knock on the door.

Salim came in and kissed me. "How are you?" he asked. "I hope all is well. You certainly look lovely. I am thrilled to see you."

I asked him about his day. He smiled but did not bother to answer.

He slid the robe I was wearing off me. He took my hand

and said, "Come, I want to lie with you."

It sounded almost biblical. It was what I wanted too. I had waited for this moment, to see Salim again, and to spend time together. We lay down on the bed and talked a bit. I told Salim about my day, my time with the dolphins, the cheeky goat who made its way into my garden and watched me as I swam naked in the private pool. I told him I thought it was him, reincarnated as a pushy goat, coming to check up on me. He said, "It was me, and now I am coming back to get what I saw in the sunshine and to enjoy all of it after dark."

He rolled out of chatting mode position and was ready to move into a different type of communication altogether. He kissed me for some time, and the slipped off his dish-dash.

He was smiling down on me while working me with his nimble fingers.

Salim locked his black eyes onto mine. We were in the missionary position.

Very appropriate, I chuckled to myself. *It had been Salim's mission to get me into bed. Mission accomplished.*

Salim hovered above me and slowly came into me, making sure I was OK. When he felt comfortable that I was too, he picked up the pace. As he increased the rhythm of his thrusts, he kept looking at me with those dark eyes and whispered,

"Last night was good. Did you enjoy it? Would you like something else to remember me by?"

"Yes, I would," I whispered.

"Your wish is my command and my utter pleasure," he breathed.

While still expertly working me, he asked, "Have you ever got entangled in a threesome?"

"No, never," I replied, adding "but I may consider it."

He slowed down and looked at me intently. "Go on," he said.

"Well," I responded, "I have a friend who is up for that sort of thing."

"She is discreet," I said breathlessly, as he increased his rhythm. "She is reliable and very good at what she does."

"Tell me," he mumbled as he performed most excellently.

"Her name is Jessica. She is curved in all the right places," I whispered.

"She wears nothing but eight strings of snow-white pearls around her neck. When she is turned on, she wiggles and jiggles and touches every spot you would like her to."

My breath faltered. His eyes looked like two sizzling coals in his sculpted face.

They were burning with lust and anticipation. Salim picked up the pace again and took full control, his nostrils flaring.

I teased him a little more. "If we were having a threesome, what position would you be in?" Without hesitation and locking his full attention on me, he gave me his sardonic smile and mumbled, "Pole Position. I will always be in Pole Position."

"What a cocky shit," I thought. "What a delicious cocky shit." Then he thrust three more times and came, shouting "Ay Yay Yay Yay", a call I had not come across before but a clear sign of release which appealed to me.

Raw and sexual. I, too, was satisfied. And happy. I liked this man.

He rolled off me. I snuggled up to him, stroking his soft skin. It is a sign of a wealthy, well-cared-for man. The skin has benefited from endless massages, the most refined oils and the most lavish body-scrubs money can buy.

We must have lain there for some hours, talking, kissing, laughing and feeling comfortable and at ease.

Then he looked at me and said, "You are pure honey. You are no doubt, very good for my health. I would eat you every day for breakfast if I had my way.

You, my Princess, are my idea of wonderful."

He turned back to the subject of Jessica.

"So, this friend of yours," he said as he nuzzled my neck, "when will we get together?"

I said that Jessica was banned from the Middle East and that we would have to wait till we were both in London.

I said that Jessica was "all about sex". "A rampant, royal fuck you could depend on".

And that she was. Always ready to play at the switch of a button. Jessica was easy. No strings attached. Literally. But I decided not to reveal any further details on the potential meeting.

I smiled up at him, from under his arm, where he held me. I loved that snug spot.

"*Shu Habibti?*" he said "What, sweetie?"

"Nothing," I said. I lay with Salim in comfortable silence.

Then he kissed me on the forehead and got up. He headed for the shower.

I could hear him switching on my electric toothbrush. I liked the fact that he did not ask. He simply used it.

Then I heard him as he turned on the tropical rain forest shower, the full blast of water hitting the marble. Five minutes later, he came out, still dripping.

He picked up his dish-dash and was about to put it on over his wet body.

I looked at him quizzically. "Shall I get you a towel?" I asked him.

"No need, Gorgeous One, but thank you for the offer. I never dry myself after a shower.

I dress and go. I am drip dry, after all."

Still damp, but now fully dressed, Salim took me in his arms and kissed me softly.

He lifted my chin with his index finger and gave me a gentle tap on the nose.

Then he flashed me that his scintillating and irresistible smile. With a twinkle in his eye, he said, "See you in London. I will be looking forward to that tremendously." He kissed me one more time, turned towards the door and left.

Not knowing what to do after his departure, I went for a long, hot shower.

When I finished and returned to the room, there was a message flashing on the phone.

I listened to the mailbox.

It was Salim. In his dark dulcet tones, he said, "I have loved getting to know you, Ms Vivi Vivacious, or should I say, Ms Very Delicious. You have the touch. I welcome you on board and look forward to close collaborations with you. See you in London.

I am looking forward to having you, and if you like, Jessica. Be good. Sweet dreams."

Best Kept Secret

Back in the London office, things were in turmoil.
One of the staff fought with another, causing all matter of follow-on interviews with the Human Resources director. Sophie, my P.A., was deeply distressed, as she had lost her cat two days earlier, and made no attempt to try and do any work.

Redhead was stressed, as she was waiting for contracts from Asia, which were overdue.

Most things could have been addressed, resolved, or even avoided, but there was no forward-thinking, little planning and always drama of one sort or another.

Undeniably, the most enjoyable part of my day was when "His Truly", called.

His fun, and more often than not, brilliant conversation, was a welcome counterbalance to the work.

At weekends, we would chat for hours, but also regularly just connected for fifteen minutes, during the day. We often talked, mostly when he was at one of his resorts, or on one of his long drives.

I got to know about his past. I was enchanted by the stories about his childhood in the desert. He told me about one of his homes, which he built in the place where he grew up, to keep his childhood memories alive, in The Empty Quarter of Oman.

Salim was a very hard-working, as well as a highly sociable man. Switching off for him was a rare occurrence. He enjoyed other people's company, good food and wine, conversation, and humour. As a result, he was hardly ever, if ever, alone.

People gravitated towards him. As much as he could be harsh and outspoken, he could be utterly charismatic.

Back in the day, he must have been quite a ladies' man. He could charm the pants off even the most defiant, opinionated person if he put his mind to it. Of that, I was living proof.

Sometimes, when he called me, he let on that perhaps he could do with some time to himself. The only part of the day or night that he was able to have total peace and quiet was when he was in his own bedroom, which he did not share with his wife.

I learnt that it is considered quite normal and expected that the husband and wife get together for sex or lovemaking, depending on the relationship. After their union, they typically both go their separate ways and occupy their own bedrooms. I must say that arrangement immensely appealed to me in principle. While I could not think of anything more divine than to snuggle up after intimate and glorious lovemaking, I also liked the idea of having my own space and not having to share the same bed with someone every day. You would then not be troubled by snoring, the difference in room temperature preferences and other incompatibilities that there may be.

Mulling over my musings, I realised that this man would

never live anywhere with me. He didn't even reside on my continent. Our existences were worlds apart.

I had not mentioned Salim to anyone, not even to my Pussy Posse, though I think they may have had their suspicions there was a love interest; still, they did not push me. He was my best-kept secret.

I needed to be in Dubai for an important client meeting, so I contacted Salim.

"Hi, Salim, I am so excited to be coming to Dubai, but it will only be for twenty-four hours."

"Hi, Princess, great news. The minute you land, I will have you picked up. You will come straight to my office. I know you need to see clients, but before that, you need to see "your owner"," he teased.

And that is what I did. We spent some hours together and agreed to see each other that evening. I met with the clients. I managed to land the contract we were working on.

Due to the clients' office location, I was staying in one of the older five-star hotels in town, on Sheikh Zayed Road. Salim was pleased when I told him. The reason was that he would be less likely to bump into anyone he knew. All his family, friends and associates typically frequented the latest, most lush and lavish hotels in town. The hotel where I was staying was one of the first hotels built on Sheikh Zayed Road and was now considered "passé". I didn't mind. It was a fleeting visit.

After I returned to the hotel, I took my time getting dressed. I wore one of my favourite ankle-length dresses with swirls of emerald, tangerine, and turquoise. It had a deep V-neckline, that allowed a glimpse of bosom, without being too revealing.

I applied some make-up, and I went into the elevator to go up to the restaurant, located on the top floor.

As the door opened, he was right there, taking the same elevator up.

There were other people in the lift, so he didn't say anything apart from a polite "good evening", but the minute he laid his eyes on me, I saw that look come over him; the one that spells H.O.R.N.Y.

We both stepped out on the top floor. Salim brushed my boob, grinned at me, and said:

"How are you, V? You look spectacular."

"I am good, S. I am happy to see you," I replied.

"Me too," he said and squeezed my hand discreetly.

"You never know who may be watching," he whispered. "You are my "forbidden fruit", my "passion fruit"."

We were seated at the best table in the sky lounge restaurant, with a great view of Dubai. We had some great "surf and turf", a combination of seafood and steak.

As always, the conversation flowed, and I was happy. Time flew by. I loved talking to him and being in his company.

"What would you like for dessert, Princess?" he said softly. He handed me the menu.

I glanced at the card and dismissed it.

"I can't see what I want on the menu," I said in a sultry voice. "Are you sure there isn't anything you would like for dessert?" he urged.

"I want something sweet, but it is not on the menu," I flirted. Salim's eyes noticeably darkened and glistened.

"Give me your room number," he said. "I will get the bill and meet you there."

I slid out of my seat and left the restaurant and went to my room. I waited for Salim, leaving the door ajar, so he could come to slip straight in without having to spend any more time than necessary in the corridor.

Everywhere you go in Dubai there are cameras. Making an inconspicuous entry was needed. The last thing this man wanted was to be caught red-handed on camera, in a less than seven-star hotel, with a woman who was not his wife.

Salim came in and wasted no time in slipping between the sheets.

He made passionate love to me. Then, as was his way, he cradled me against him.

As I lay there, where I felt so right, I realised that in this part of the world, nothing could be considered more wrong. The reality was that you could be stoned to death for being with a married man.

How could such ancient tribal traditions still be enforceable, in such a seemingly modern place?

Redhead Rebellion

I could hear Shannon rant. "She is too close to him. Is she working for him or us?"

Her shrill and tense voice was clearly audible through my office window.

I had been out, attending a client meeting. I returned, but Shannon hadn't realised.

"Redhead" was clearly on the line to someone her senior. The CEO, I thought.

"Yes," she screamed in a high pitch, "I know she was able to get General Salim to allow us to add Turtle Island Resort to our portfolio and I know that was a big deal, but I am her boss. He does not employ Vivika. I am getting frustrated being side-lined like this, and I don't think it is right that this is allowed to continue."

And with that, I closed the window with a bang. Shannon must have realised it was me. Her voice trailed off.

Just then, the phone rang. "Hi, V." I forgot everything and answered.

"Hi, S."

"How are these incompetent so and so's treating you?"

"Well," I said, "I just overheard a disconcerting conversation, that does not bode well."

"Tell me what happened," he said.

Just then, Shannon knocked on the door and walked straight into my office.

"May I call you back?" I hung up without waiting for his reply. I knew he would realise that something was amiss.

Shannon mentioned nothing about her conversation, part of which I had clearly overheard.

She went straight into the topic of tomorrow's five a.m. conference call with the team in Asia. She started babbling on about a contract that she couldn't find and a paper she had misplaced. She was ranting on, and my mind went to those conference calls.

I didn't mind the timing so much as the time it took. Those calls occurred every week. No progress of consequence was made. I found it utterly infuriating. No wonder Boss-Man, or "my man", as I now called him, to myself only, was so frustrated.

"So," Shannon said, "what do you think we should do?"

My mind must have totally wandered, as I had no clue what she was referring to.

That was bad. I should have listened to what Shannon had been going on about. My mind was elsewhere.

I thought on my feet. As Shannon, was looking down at her notes, I purposefully brushed the half-full coffee cup off my desk. It hit the floor and broke. The cold remains went flying across the office carpet and door.

"Oh no, so sorry," I said, "let me get a cloth." When I came back, she was gone.

I never did find out what she was asking my thoughts on.

I was happy when I finally got home.

As I settled on to the sofa with a cup of tea, I saw my phone light up.

My heart did a little leap of joy. It was him. The message read, "V, where the devil are you? How is that delicious V between your legs? In excellent working and good order, as I remember it, I hope".

My loins stirred. Salim knew how to press my buttons, even from continents away. I felt puss responding instantly.

"Don't start what you can't finish," I replied. "And don't tease me just to entice me. That is just not elegant, fair, or appropriate." This was followed by a smiley face.

"What sort of a day are you having?" he messaged back. "Hope all is well".

I decided not to discuss the day.

What to say? Should I tell him that Redhead and Co. are upset, that we get on so well? And that they think I have more influence over you than they do? What was the point? He may get annoyed and give "Rotten Redhead", an even tougher ride. I had once asked him why he always insisted on giving Shannon such a hard time.

He just grinned at me and said, "I would never choose to give her a hard time. She is not worthy of anything hard to be wasted on her. She is infuriating and incompetent and utterly useless."

"In her defence, she is not stupid or ugly," I said.

"Maybe not, but those shoulders are so big that she looks like an Olympic swimming rugby player. She is disproportionate, and her skin is not just white, it is brighter than my dish-dash fresh from the dry-cleaners. She should always keep her clothes on," he went on, "and not attempt sex under any conditions or circumstances unless it is with cave-dwellers. Maybe when they are done chewing on raw bones and are looking for something to get their savage teeth into, then, and only then, would that Rotten Redhead, experience a man's mouth on any part of her despicable body."

I laughed, choking on my Earl Grey tea in a less than lady-like fashion.

"You, my friend," I responded, "appear to be an elegant, eloquent and well-bred individual, but you are the devil incarnate."

Salim made me laugh with his outrageous comments and extreme political incorrectness. He amused the socks off me. He was sharp and astute in his observations. His scathing and callous remarks could kill, while his words of wisdom and kindness, could soothe. It just depended on what, and whom, he was dealing with, and in which context.

Salim, eight years my senior, was wise, competent, and go-getting. He was tough and determined. Salim did not suffer fools gladly. He had a kind and softer side, which most people never got to see.

AJ and his entire family experienced Salim's compassion first-hand.

Even though he barked at Zeina, she too, found protection when needed. Her fierce loyalty to General Salim never wavered.

The phone rang. "What is going on, Young Lady?" Salim said.

"Nothing much. It's been a busy, weird kind of day. I am glad it is over."

"Anything I can help with, Princess?"

"You can always help me with one thing," I flirted, "but that typically needs me to be in your vicinity."

"Soon, you will be," he said. "We will make it happen."

"I have to dash out to a family function, but before going out, I just wanted to check up on you. I have to head out to my wife's sister. I bought them all houses some time back. Now they seem to think they have to invite me. Kind enough people, but I fancy a night in my home. For some reason, I seem to be a bit low on energy. Not sure why but, hey ho, as they say. Must dash."

He then waited for me to add my usual, "Dash in your dish- dash," which I did.

I could hear him smile down the phone.

I went on to say, "Thanks for checking up on me," adding, "It's not like you to be off colour. Maybe you have been burning the candle at both ends."

"Not sure what it is. It will pass. Sending kisses for you and puss. Catch you later, Princess".

With that, he rang off.

Jessica Jeopardy

Next morning when I got up, as a joke, I took a picture of Jessica, who was lying on my bed.

Jessica was short for Jessica Rabbit, a pink vibrator designed with the progressive woman in mind. When turned on, she leapt into a swirling dance, meant for internal use.

Finally, Salim would know "what", rather than "who", Jessica was.

Feeling exuberant and upbeat, I took a picture of Jessica, attached it to his email address, and pressed "send".

I chuckled to myself, knowing he would laugh and at the same time, be turned on.

He would respond instantly, the minute he would see this perfect pink dildo in his inbox, soon to be inserted into mine, when he was next in London.

Within seconds, I felt gut-wrenchingly sick and instantly dizzy.

I realised, too late, that I had sent the photo of my pink vibrator to the company group email, rather than to Salim's Hotmail.

OMG! What to do?

I panicked. How could I recall the email? I felt sick and faint and couldn't think.

My head was spinning, my gut turning. I knew there was only one thing for it. I had to call him.

He answered within the second ring and greeted me, seemingly full of beans,

"Good morning, Princess, my brightest Sunshine, what a lovely day it is."

"No! I let out. No, it is not! I have just sent you a photo of Jessica to your company email and Zeina will see it. I am so sorry! Don't know what to say."

"I have to go," he said abruptly, "to sort this out." And he was gone.

I sank to the floor. "No, no, no, please, no!" I shouted out loud. "This is so bad! OMG!"

I wanted to vomit, to wake up from this utter nightmare. But it was done.

All I could think of was to send a message to Zeina, saying that I sent a virus-infected message and to please not open it.

My God, I don't know whether she would or whether she had. I will never see him again.

The world seemed to collapse around me.

A simple joke, a bit of naughtiness, meant to evoke a giggle. No harm intended. It was all just too awful to contemplate. And why?

Because once again, I acted before thinking, swept up in the notion that this was fun and edgy. But it backfired most horrifically. I was about to lose it all…

I could do nothing but slump on the bed, where Jessica still lay. I hurtled Jessica through the open door, into the bathroom. I could not stand the sight of her.

Had it not been for Jessica, I would not be in this mess.

After what seemed like a very long time, Salim called. He told me what he did, following my phone call, alerting him to the Jessica incident. Salim had gone into Ms Efficiency's office and caused a scene. He shouted and said that he was outraged. "Out! Out!" he yelled at the team.

The staff trembled in their boots. The Boss erupted in great fury, without any discernible reason. Zeina had no idea what had happened and was utterly confused.

Salim went into the company email and found my message, with the photo of Jessica attached. Before deleting it, he sent it to his own personal Hotmail account "to enjoy", as he told me later. Then he emptied the trash, deleted all traces, and stomped off to his office, instructing whoever was around that he did not wish to be disturbed.

His conversation with me was short.

He said he had dealt with the matter and did not want to arouse suspicions.

Until this very day, the Jessica Saga still makes me feel sick to my core.

It taught me an unforgettable lesson.

Always think twice and check three times before you press "send".

It seemed disaster was diverted, for the moment, at least. I was relieved, Salim had not banned me from his life.

Though, I could have understood it if he had.

His reputation, his commercial empire, and his family, were all at stake.

I had a shower and tried to sleep after a most horrifically awful day.

I checked my inbox.

There it was; an email from Salim. My heart skipped a beat. I read on.

He wrote, "Vivika, I hope you had a good night's sleep and feel relaxed. I played whatever role to overcome the situation yesterday with the Jessica incident. However, this should teach both of us to be more careful. I am married and have kids. While I enjoy each second we spend, I cannot neglect my family situation, or your professional position, for that matter. I am no angel, but in my part of the world, I must be extremely careful. Since the Jessica incident, Zeina will be watching. Please communicate personal matters to my Hotmail, from your Hotmail only. Take care and take it easy. You, Jessica & I will have a great time in August".

I replied, "Thank you for taking the time to write to me. I treasure our friendship and yes, love spending time with you. Don't want to break anything, least of all what matters most, what is done with genuine feelings, and should not destroy, but add to both our lives. I hope we are friends forever. And lovers when we can".

I poured myself a glass of water and contemplated the events of the past twenty-four hours. The inevitable had occurred. Our bubble was about to burst. I teared up, then smiled through my tears, because of Salim saying that he enjoyed spending every second with me. And I knew he did.

He told people that he adored me, that I was a breath of fresh air.

We got on like a house on fire, a fire that was about to spiral out of control: it could destroy everything in its wake.

A massive sense of foreboding came over me.

In the Dark

I arrived at the office bright and early. I liked being there before anyone else.

This was my chance to get some work done and typically to have a quick good morning chat with Salim, after his office meeting and before his day was in full swing.

After the "Jessica Incident", Salim and I agreed that he would call me, not vice versa. That way, he could better control the situation and continue our communication.

Every quarter, Salim chaired Board Meetings. On those days he would start at seven a.m. and continue well into the early evening. These times were extra hectic work-wise for him. On those days, he would not be able to call. I respected his time and these work responsibilities and just lay low. Usually, I would receive a voice note or a quick "Hi".

I knew he would re-emerge soon enough.

Today must be one of those days, though he usually let me know when he had all-day meetings and could not connect.

I poured my second cup of freshly brewed coffee.

Team members started to trickle in. The day went by in an uneventful manner. I realised how much I missed it if I didn't hear from Salim.

I had become accustomed to his attention, messages, and interactions. I had fallen for this man.

Around lunchtime, something was going on around the office.

"Have you heard?" Sophie said.

"Heard what?" I asked.

"We are not sure precisely what is going on, but I happened to have Zeina on the phone just now. She said she had to go, as General Salim was in the hospital and there was no time to waste."

"In the hospital?" My gut turned upside down. I felt sick. I tried to keep my emotional response under control and said, "That doesn't sound good. What is up?"

"I have no idea," she said. "Hope he will be OK, though it will take some pressure off us if he is not around. Long may it continue." She grinned and immediately realised the error of her ways.

"Sophie!" I reprimanded her sharply. "What an inconsiderate and outrageous thing to say." Her cheeks flushed bright red.

"I am so sorry. Please forgive me," she stammered.

Sophie may well have wondered why I had reacted so sharply to her comment. I was on edge and worried. I could not think of anything else other than Salim.

I told the team to meet in my office. Daily discussions and refreshed minds were needed, with focus on our goals. It would also keep me from slipping into a panic, possibly causing suspicion. I kept my cool for as long as needed.

At the end of the brief morning meeting, I told Sophie not to allow any disturbances unless they were urgent calls.

I closed the door and opened the window. What to do?

I could not contact him as, no doubt, his wife and or family would be with him.

I felt sad, desperate and lost. Our communication could only take place in secret.

What if something terrible had happened?

I did not sleep. I couldn't bear it.

I sent a reasonably general sounding email to Ms Efficiency. "Dear Zeina", I wrote, "I hope you are well. We are all concerned to hear that General Salim was taken ill. We hope he will be in good health again soon. Please pass on our sincere good wishes for a speedy recovery. Best wishes, The London Team".

No answer that afternoon. The hours dragged on and on.

At around six o'clock in the evening, there was a message from Zeina.

"Thank you, Miss Vivika", it read. "I am not able to update you on General Salim. He has been flown to London, where specialists will examine him. I will keep you up to date when I can. For now, just concentrate on the business. As you know, if the company does well, it will help him recover more quickly. Regards".

My heart was racing; my head was spinning. What was going on? I could not connect with him, visit him, care for him, see him.

Word had it that General Salim was very wealthy. One day, I had a very heated conversation about our relationship, or lack of it, shall we say. I blurted out to him,

"I don't give a monkey's ass about your towers, your condos, your resorts, your hospitals or anything. I care about you, and that is all."

He locked his eyes onto me, looking at me pleadingly, taking my hands in his.

"I know, Vivi. You and I, we are one on one. Nothing beyond us matters. I utterly adore you. I wish it were different, but I am married and have commitments which I cannot deny or ignore". He then pulled me into him, kissed the crown of my head and stroked my hair, as I sobbed my loving heart out against his chest. I knew he would never be mine.

"Ping". That soundbite, that brings you back from your thoughts to the current time and place. It was an email from the CEO. It read, "Vivika, there is a trade fair that is taking place in Chicago. I was supposed to go, but in the circumstances, I need you to be on the flight tomorrow afternoon. You will be there for four days. Kindly confirm".

What were the chances? Just as Salim was being flown to London, I would be off to Chicago. Damn.

There was nothing to do but get on with it. I confirmed and started packing.

Having prepared my bag, I decided to send Salim a message from my other phone.

I would send the message from "Team London", conveying formal best wishes from the company for a speedy recovery. After some time, I could see that the note had been read. But by whom? There was no response.

I woke up to my phone ringing. I did not recognise the caller I.D. But saw it was a local number. I answered.

In a barely audible voice, I heard him whisper, "I am alive. I wanted you to know. Don't call."

It sounded like he had mustered every ounce of his energy to say what he had. Then everything went dead.

I was knocked sideways and in shock. I felt like I was being sucked into a vortex.

My disbelief swirling like liquid around an axis of relief. Salim sounded as if he were at death's door. His voice was frail and faint. He barely seemed able to utter those few words to me, mere minutes ago. What on earth could be the case? I hoped to God that Salim would stay with me on this earth.

The Chicago trade-fair came and went. Days turned into nights and nights into weeks.

At work, they did not know their ass from their elbow. It was tedious to watch and painful to see such potential possibilities turn to waste through incompetence and irrational action.

All things sexy lose their thrill when they do not have a foundation of intelligence or substance.

I knew I could not stay with this company, no matter how I felt about General Salim.

I tried to stay busy and focused, but my heart and mind were elsewhere. Salim told me not to contact him, which I tried, with all my resolve.

But eventually, I couldn't bear it any longer. The pressure was too much to take. The need to connect too strong to ignore.

I limited myself to send a short message every nine days. At those times, my aching heart would spill out poetry, about little ships sinking, though they had been intended to float.

Some of my writings, I erased. They were more like therapy for the soul. I expressed my loss, in ways I could only do to myself and for myself. After all, nobody knew my love nor my pain.

I didn't know if he was able to open his email, let alone to read or press delete. Maybe someone else was reading them and pressing delete or blocking my messages.

I felt an overwhelming sense of loss and sadness; the profound disorientation that comes from not knowing.

After endless weeks, I slowly and painfully resigned myself to the fact that what had been was no more. I forced myself to ignore my troubled heart and use my brain instead. I tried to accept the things I did not have the power to change.

I tried to respect myself and to move on.

Omens & Signs

The company was in decline; the auditors were called in. There was talk of hostile take-overs. The atmosphere was depressing and without hope.

I sent my c.v. to several head-hunters in London, Canada and the U.S., who recruited for international hotel chains.

I wrote my resignation letter to the CEO, the captain of this sinking ship. I personally and repeatedly, experienced his lack of backbone and resolve. *Yet another spineless "Mr. Blobby".*

I re-read the email once. With a sense of purpose, as well as relief, I pressed "send".

I decided to go for a drive. It was a chilly yet sunshiny day. I put the roof down on the convertible. Being in the beautiful countryside lifted my spirits to a degree. I decided to stop for lunch in a pub. The Chablis was crisp and cold, the salad delicious, and the fish grilled to perfection.

No matter how delectable and nutritious the food was, my soul remained starving and parched, hungry and thirsty for news of Salim.

Having driven randomly across the countryside, I returned home and parked the car in the driveway next to the house. I sat perfectly still, not wanting to move.

Then, something inexplicable and totally bizarre occurred. A moment in time etched in my memory. It was poignant and powerful.

Whilst I was on Turtle Island, I had bought a gorgeous bracelet, in the exquisite island boutique. It was made from genuine turquoise stone, shaped into beads, with a small silver dolphin pendant, dancing off it. I was instantly drawn to the piece. It somehow symbolised a connection with Salim.

It was unique, striking, perfectly crafted and wildly different from anything I had ever seen before. I had been wearing it pretty much nonstop since my trip to the Maldives.

For some reason, I had taken it off whilst I was driving. It had somehow irritated me and felt uncomfortable. I placed it in the little money tray between the seats in the car.

I arrived home and parked. I took the key out of the ignition, when suddenly and dramatically, the bracelet exploded, sending the beads flying through the car.

I hadn't touched the bangle. It sprung apart entirely of its own accord, as if a powerful force had blown a fuse. The only way for the energy to go was outward.

"What just happened?" I said out loud, utterly bewildered.
Wow! If ever there was a sign, an omen, this was it.
How should I interpret it? Release of negative energy? A new beginning?
Or…, suddenly my heart stopped.
Did Salim die and was this him letting me know he had gone?

I sat for a moment, holding the steering wheel, trying to calm and compose myself. Then, a slow but sure steadiness came over me, putting me in a state of deep peace. The sense of balance and calm can only be described as grounding.

I subliminally knew that everything would be alright.

I was on the early train, going into London for an interview. I had decided to leave the sinking ship, but now needed to, once again, secure a new job.

I was trying to recall how many weeks it had been since I heard from Salim.

Was it five or six weeks now, since Salim called me from the hospital, struggling to tell me that he was still alive?

Days and dates seem to merge, without significance or purpose. There was a deep and painful void in my life where Salim had been. Not being able to speak to him, being cut off from his energy and entire being, was like forced fasting. I felt starved and depleted. It was excruciating and painful.

I sat on the train as it sped smoothly down the track.

It was still dark outside. The days were cold, gloomy and dull. I was thinking of Salim, so intently. Even after all these weeks, I could make myself believe he was right there, that he was physically by my side. I looked at my reflection in the window of the train, as we sped through a long dark tunnel when something miraculous happened.

There was a sudden, forceful, and intense golden glow, that seemed to embrace my heart. It softly hugged me, like a shimmering cloud of warmth. Little sparkling gold-coloured mosaic energy fragments formed and swirled around me.

A deep and meaningful wave of extreme positivity engulfed me.

I had never experienced anything like this. I knew it was Salim.

You are still here. Thank God.

My heart started to breathe. It's shrivelled chambers, devoid of life and oxygen, seemed to be re-inflating, the blood started pumping, allowing joy to begin to trickle back into my heart.

I had no idea where Salim was. But I knew he was alive.

Soul Synergy

My first day on the new job was arranging a pop-up shop in the West Country.

This social enterprise imported hand-made goods from the Middle East.

On my way West to the event, I received a message. I stopped the car in the motorway lay-by.

It was Salim! My heart missed a beat.

The message simply said, "Please call me when you can".

While I found it impossibly tempting to jump straight on a call and speak to Salim, I texted him back saying, "Hope all OK. Happy to hear from you. Today is the first day of a new job. Can I call when I finish tomorrow afternoon?".

The reason I did not phone back immediately was that I knew I would be thrown off balance and have only him on my mind. Having resigned from my other job, I absolutely had to make this one work.

Not to mention the fact that I had not heard from him for all these weeks, without knowing precisely what happened. After the excruciating pain I went through, I had to protect myself.

I needed to be strong enough and not throw myself back into the whirlpool, which almost drowned me.

"Talk tomorrow", he texted back.

Naturally, I was discombobulated. After all this time, I had heard from Salim. He was suddenly back within reach. With great resolve, I went ahead and did what was needed.

We set up the pop-up shop, arranged for the catering, and went through the play-book for the day. Then, the green carpet, literally a carpet of grass, was laid.

The place looked a treat.

Having worked an eighteen-hour day, we ate some light snacks and slept, only to be up early again the next day to run the event.

We did good business and received excellent PR coverage. Having finished a successful mission, we completed the team-debrief and wrapped up. I put my bag in the car, and set off back eastwards, on the drive home.

Realising that I had not thought continuously about Salim, pleased me.

It made me think that I was able to manage my response to him. I was now free and, in a position, to dial his number. Instead, I decided, I would call him in an hour or so, not merely at the first opportunity. I had to practice some resolve and build the muscle of protection.

Just as I was planning to call Salim in an hour, my mobile rang. It was him. He beat me to it. I stopped the car in the lay-by to answer and plugged in my headphones.

Then I set off on the journey home.

It was the first time after countless, desperate weeks that I heard his voice.

"Vivika," he said.

My stomach turned. Salim called me Vivi, Princess, Sunshine, or whatever, but never my complete Christian name, "Vivika". "Are you OK?" I asked, in a soft voice. I was happy to hear him, though, at the same time, uneasy and unsure of how to conduct myself.

"Vivi. Listen to me. Do not speak until I have finished. Do not interrupt me until I have totally completed what I want to tell you. Do not intrude, stop me, or say a word. Promise me that."

"I promise," I said, feeling both confused and on high alert.

It was quiet on his side for several seconds. I could hear him lighting a cigarette and inhaling. Then Salim spoke.

"I want to apologise."

I was thrown. I don't think this man ever apologised to anyone. Certainly not as long as I had known him. Nor could I ever imagine Salim feeling remorse, or guilt about any choices he made in his life or career.

I was about to say something, then bit my tongue.

He continued. "I have not been in touch after that day I called you from the hospital. I was very ill indeed. I almost died. I kept my distance during my recovery. My family found out about us. As I told you before, I was no angel. I said to myself that I should ignore you, cut you out and not pose any threats to my family. But I was wrong. I ask you to forgive me. It was short-sighted and small-minded of me, to think that by staying silent, our friendship and relationship would die. Please forgive me. I am so very sorry that I have not been in touch, and that I left you, not knowing and not hearing from me.

Forgive me, Vivi."

I was lost for words. I opened the window to let in some fresh air.

When I thought he had finished, I said, "Now may I speak?"

"Yes," he said.

"I am glad you are OK. I am so happy you are back. I am very sorry for what you have gone through. The past six weeks have been some of the worst of my life, not knowing what was happening to you."

I welled up, as I felt the unhealed hurt and sadness I had experienced over the past weeks, rising to the surface. I took a deep breath and continued, "I respect your position with regards to your family. Clearly, we don't exist in a bubble, and circumstances were already against us. We will fit together in whatever way God intended. If this is as a friend, I will be grateful. You are nothing like anybody I have ever met. After God made you, He broke the mould."

Salim was so attuned to me that he knew, I was softly choking on my pain.

"My Vivi," he said softly. "My dearest Vivi, I am so deeply sorry for the hurt I have caused you."

Salim then surprised me, as he recited one of my favourite French quotes, by an anonymous poet.

"Je voudrais être une larme.

Pour naître dans tes yeux. Vivre sur tes joues. Et mourir sur tes lèvres".

I could not believe what I was hearing.

Then, repeating the same words, translated, infusing humour, Salim in exaggerated poetic fashion, said, "I would so like to be a teardrop, to be born in your sparkling green, blue eyes. To live on your gorgeous rosy cheeks, and to die on those kissable lips, that I have missed so much".

Salim was not particularly into arts or poetry, or French. However, he was definitely into pooling all his resources to achieve what was needed. In this case, his mission was to make me feel better.

Salim's unexpected and mind-blowing poem recital both surprised and somehow relaxed me. He picked up on my response.

"Good girl, Vivi. Let me hear that smile."

"Where the hell did you learn the French lines?" I blurted out.

"I recall you reciting it to me one day. I did not really understand what the hell you were saying at the time, but you translated it for me. My French is shoddy. However, I had a lot of time on my hands during my weeks in the hospital and while in recovery. When I thought of you, the verse came to mind. I looked it up and memorised it. And here we are. It came in usefully. It cheered you up. You deserve to always be happy, Princess."

Feeling more like myself again, I set off on a seemingly random train of thought, and said, "It is amazing really, isn't it? that the body has a built-in fuse-box".

"How do you mean?" Salim asked, sounding both intrigued and entertained.

He knew that, as I had started to talk, my mental state had improved.

I could hear from his voice that my feeling better positively impacted on him too.

"Well," I started, "When you are feeling angry or distraught, you cry.

When you are overjoyed, you also cry, but then you shed

tears of joy.

And when you are having great sex, pleasure builds. When it can't go any further, then like a wave, it spills over into ecstasy, through orgasm. So that is amazing, isn't it?

In the end, it all must come out. It is life's longing to express itself. If you don't release and relieve the pressure, you would simply explode, or become very ill, and you may be eaten away from the inside."

"V, I missed that magic, mad mind of yours. No one on this planet comes out with your thoughts, platitudes, crazy ideas and poignant insights. Always stay true to you. Don't ever change. You, my Princess, are a breath of fresh air. And I, for one, feel I can breathe again".

"Now, who is the poet?" I quipped.

We both laughed. As if nothing happened, our energies reconnected seamlessly. We conversed like nothing had come between us.

We talked about how Salim felt in his darkest hours, in hospital.

Salim told me he thought he was going to die. Lying there in the dark, in the middle of the night, with the lights of the machines flashing, when he was totally alone, he thought a lot about many things.

He was absolutely determined to survive and to see his son graduate.

Salim told me that if life had death in store for him, he would have to accept it. But not before Said, one of his twin boys, graduated.

Determined and driven, Salim, battled and eventually pulled through. He managed, albeit in a wheelchair, to attend the ceremony at the Royal Military Academy, Sandhurst in the UK. Salim was grateful to have been in hospital in London, so his chances of being able to attend were improved. Had he been in Oman or the US, there would have been no way to have attended.

"It must have been amazing to be back after all these years," I said.

"Yes, I remember those days well. Before I joined SOAF, the Sultanate of Oman Airforce, which later became RAFO, the Royal Airforce Oman, I graduated from Sandhurst.

It was a proud moment indeed to see Said follow in my footsteps. For good or for bad," he joked, but I could hear his pride in his voice.

"I know I had to retire from the Air Force some years after I became General due to a health condition. I was distressed at the time, but I have to say, Vivi, there was an upside. I learned all about the world of business and investments. I enjoy it. Most of the time, that is. More importantly, had I still been in the Royal Air Force, our paths would never have crossed, I would imagine. In that case, my Princess, I would not have enjoyed some of the most precious times in my life. The ones I spent with you."

"Charmer," I said, as his words made me well up.

We continued talking about his health scare, his wife and others finding out about "us".

Before I knew it, the three-hour car-journey had passed, and I was back in my neck of the woods.

After my long conversation with Salim, I felt I could breathe again.

All the things we wanted to say were said.

As I pulled into the drive and parked, I said, "I arrived home."

"Me too," he replied. "Let's meet tomorrow at our favourite place in SW3, Vivi."

"I can't think of anything I would like more," I said, adding, "Be generous with the Oud. I have not inhaled that scent on you for so long."

I could hear his silent smile.

"Can't wait to see you, V," followed by, "Must dash."

"Must dash in your dish-dash," I responded, smiling.

"Ciao Princess," he laughed.

"Bye S," I said.

We hung up at the same time. We were back in sync.

The Next Chapter

I called for an extra-ordinary online meeting with The Pussy- Posse.

I knew that Annie, Hélène and Priscilla were concerned about me, but I had not been ready to share, until now.

We caught up. I explained in not too much detail, why I had gone AWOL (Absent Without Official Leave - a military term, James jokingly used to use when I had not seen him for a while). The girls asked me to never again suffer alone, though we all agreed that every now and then, you just have to deal with circumstances by yourself. Not everything can always be shared when you find yourself in the eye of the storm.

We renewed our vows. "Through thick and thin and through sick and sin," we swore. Then we planned our next "Pussy Posse Get Together".

I poured myself a G&T, sat back on my favourite sofa and reflected.

As a young girl growing up, I was incredibly independent. As I matured, without being aware of it happening, I slipped into a level of dependency. Whether it was with "my" British

Captain, or "my" Omani General, I realised that I lost myself a bit.

Both amazing men captured my imagination and held my attention. There was no doubt about that. But I gave them the central position in my life, rather than myself.

Much of the time, I acted with them in mind, allowing my world to revolve around James, and later around Salim.

While both men were significant, I realised that I had not only given my heart but my compass too.

I pondered my wisdom. I could see more clearly now.

I was happy to sing, but not to someone else's tune, even if it was a love song.

I had learned. And grown.

My true north was intact, and my personal compass firmly back with me.

I was happy. I felt more robust and more balanced. I could never have dreamed up my life's journey so far and was quite sure I would not be able to imagine what was yet to come. I was excited!

"To life and living it," I said out loud.

I was ready for "The Next Chapter".

Bring it on!

Interview with the Author

Helen Van Wengen (Britt Holland) is a citizen of the world. That sense of wonder, sharing and positivity in the joy of cultural exchanges has been poured into a series of books which in part reflect different aspects of Helen's own remarkable life.

Born in Holland, Helen's childhood was in the Netherlands, with frequent visits to the UK, before she travelled to Switzerland to study hospitality at one of the world's top Hospitality Management Schools. There, Helen was introduced to friends and cultures as they lived, learned, and forged strong global friendships.

This experience shaped the young woman's life forever and set her on a journey that would see her work in the hotel industry worldwide, particularly in Europe and the Middle East and in Central America and Asia.

Now living between Jordan and Amsterdam, Helen is engaged in multiple projects, ranging from hospitality and tourism to social enterprise initiatives that drive profit for purpose, people, and planet. Helen believes in aspirational outcomes with a positive spirit. With her upbeat nature, Helen knows that miracles happen every day.

And on meeting Helen, it is the positivity that shines through. A positivity which has enabled her to boldly reflect on complex, wonderful and sometimes frankly hilarious parts of her life for a series of fun but savvy books which have echoes of *Eat Pray Love, Sex and the City and Four Weddings and a Funeral.*

Helen said: "The journey of writing these books has been so transformational because when I am writing, I feel as though I really am there while at the same time being able to reflect on situations and emotions I write about. And in some cases, remember as the words pour out.

"There have been times that I have cried and laughed, and those elements are all in the books".

"The books are not autobiographical, but there is so much of myself and my own experiences in the characters."

And the process of writing the books she said has fuelled and developed her soul and given her great joy.

Between The Sheets is a fascinating read, full of love, drama, sex and intrigue, supported by strong female characters that give the work a sense of empowered authenticity.

Helen said: "I love how my writing has connected my heart and mind to the past, made me more conscious of each day and allows my excitement of tomorrow to spill over on to the pages of my books. As a result of writing, I reconnected with amazing friends with whom, in some cases, I lost touch. One dear friend described my books as 'a magic carpet ride' that sparked a tear, a smile, and triggered thoughts she had forgotten all about. Touching other people's lives in positive ways matters to me. I will continue to live and write stories for others as well as myself. Living life is a privilege and one I embrace.

Also by Britt Holland

Mountains of Love
A story of memories, past loves and new adventures

Vivika, the high-flying, fun-loving hospitality professional from *Between the Sheets*, attends The Grand Reunion in the Swiss Alps. Here she had lived, loved and learnt with her fellow students three decades earlier. Vivika wonders whether her old flame, Bash will attend. More than memories are rekindled on the Mountain of Love. Vivika's adventures take a turn for the worse when she is linked to an illegal trade network. Can she continue to believe in Bash, or is it time to smell the coffee? As circumstances unfold, Vivika encounters pain and gain, and sets out to write her own future.

Forever Connected
A story about good energy and forever friendships

Vivika, the hospitality professional from *Between the Sheets* who attended The Grand Reunion in *Mountains of Love*, travels to Costa Rica. Vivika finds herself co-owning a coffee plantation and meets handsome Humphrey. Against the vibrant backdrop of resplendent nature, Vivi embraces every Pura Vida day and her forever friendships. When Vivika attends the bi-annual Pussy Posse reunion in Portugal, old flame Bash, revs the powerful engine of his olive golden Aston Martin. Ready to go full throttle.

Printed in Poland
by Amazon Fulfillment
Poland Sp. z o.o., Wrocław

93212513R00169